Yasser an[d] Meet The animals in the qur'an

by ibn ali, binte abbas & friends

Sun Behind The Cloud

In the Name of Allah, the Kind, the Merciful

With special thanks to Shaykh Muhammad Saeed Bahmanpoor for checking the work for accuracy of Islamic History and Tafsir, and to Fatma Ali Jaffer for her outstanding editing.

Published by

Sun Behind The Cloud Publications Ltd

PO Box 15889, Birmingham, B16 6NZ

This edition first published in paperback 2021

A CIP catalogue record for this book is available from the British Library

ISBN (print): 978-1-908110-69-5

ISBN (ebook): 978-1-908110-70-1

www.sunbehindthecloud.com

info@sunbehindthecloud.com

  @sunbehindcloud

@sunbehindthecloud

For all those who have suffered
during the pandemic.

Let us recite a Surah Fatiha,
so the blessing brings them peace.

Share your learning
with Yasser and Zahra

If you would like to print out some of the activities, you can download them from our website:

https://www.sunbehindthecloud.com/share-your-learning-with-yasser-and-zahra

We'd love to see your work,
so please do post it on our Padlet site
(which you can find on the same link)

If you would like to send a personal message to Yasser and Zahra, you can email them on:

yasserandzahra@sunbehindthecloud.com

We're looking forward to hearing from you!

Contents

the adventure begins

Chapter 1

Zahra threw down her colouring pencils in frustration and let out a deep sigh. School had been closed for weeks because of the pandemic and all the shops were shut too. Even the bowling alley and swimming pool had locked their doors with no idea when they would open again.

Yasser walked up to Zahra's door after hearing the commotion.

"What's wrong?" he asked, taking in the chaotic scene of scattered pencils and crumpled papers.

"There's just nothing to do!" Zahra exclaimed in an exasperated tone. "This is the *third* picture I have coloured today!" she said, counting on her fingers. "I've already said my prayers, recited the Holy Qur'an and even read some books. I just don't know what else to do. I never thought I would say this, but I'm sooo bored...I wish we could go back to school!"

Yasser sighed. He knew *exactly* how Zahra was feeling. He really missed playing football with his friends, but there was a very important reason for staying indoors and he needed to remind Zahra about that. He put his arm around his little sister and Zahra leaned into his embrace. Spending so much time together had strengthened their bond; without friends and extended family, they only had each other.

"Remember *why* we are doing this," Yasser said softly.

"I know, I know..." replied Zahra, rolling her eyes. "To stay safe." She parroted the words they had heard and read countless times on the news in the past few weeks.

"We have to stay at home not only to keep ourselves safe, but also to help stop the spread of the virus," Yasser said. "If you think about it, by staying at home we're helping other people too!"

Zahra let out a long sigh. "I never thought about it like that," she said. "I just feel like I am running out of patience!"

"It's definitely a test of patience!" Yasser exclaimed, nodding his head emphatically. "I'm sure we can find something interesting to do! Let's find Grandfather and see if he has any ideas!"

Grandfather was in the prayer room reciting verses from the Holy Qur'an. When he heard the children racing down the stairs, he smiled a secret smile to himself as he waited for them to find him.

"Grandfather! Grandfather!" Yasser said, breathlessly. "We're so bored! Won't you please take us on one of your magnificent adventures?"

"*Pleeeaaaase!*" added Zahra, who had already rushed to grab the magic green rug and was holding it out. Grandfather chuckled.

"No, not this time Zahra," he said, taking the rug from her. "Let's take another kind of trip this time. Shall we try the zoo?"

"Oh no," moaned Zahra. "Not another Zoom call!"

"Not Zoom, Zahra! **THE ZOOOOOOO!**" Yasser said, chuckling.

"Ohhh. But isn't the zoo closed?" asked Zahra, confused.

"Not this one!" replied Grandfather, with a twinkle in his eye. "Freshen up and bring notebooks. I'll meet you at the front door in five minutes!"

Even though it wasn't the adventure they had thought they would be going on, Zahra and Yasser were thrilled!

"Thank you, Grandfather!" they said together, hugging him tight. Then they ran upstairs to get dressed.

"Don't forget to bring your facemasks too!" Grandfather called after them.

Grandfather went to the kitchen to prepare snacks for their trip. First, he cut some crunchy, emerald green cucumbers into wedges, then he lined up succulent sweet dates and finally he packed a few shiny black olives into a tub. Finally, he carefully poured milk and honey into two small bottles and packed those alongside the food. Happy with his work, Grandfather smiled. "These are all foods mentioned in the Holy Qur'an," he said to himself in wonder. "SubhanAllah."

As he continued remembering and praising Allah, Grandfather picked up the Holy Qur'an and went to start the car. Yasser and Zahra soon followed, notebooks in hand, as they ran to either side of the car, jumped in and slammed the doors shut simultaneously.

Zahra beamed at Yasser across the back seat. "It feels like forever since we have been anywhere," she said, quickly fastening her seatbelt. "And now we're going on one of Grandfather's adventures!"

Yasser was equally thrilled. "Alhamdullilah!" he exclaimed. "I wonder what's waiting for us this time!"

They were so excited that at first, they didn't notice that something very special (and very strange) was happening outside. The entire car had started glowing and everything around them began to shimmer. Suddenly, in a bright flash, their house and entire street disappeared and, in their place, a new road appeared in front of them!

Chapter 2

"Yasser, take this Qur'an, there is a map inside it and I need you and Zahra to read it and help me get to the zoo!" said Grandfather.

Yasser did as he was told and opened up the huge map, giving the other end to Zahra so that they could both read it.

"Drive down Baqarah Road until you come to Naml Avenue. Take a right on Naml Avenue and an immediate left onto Samak Street," Yasser read out loud.

"Then drive past Hoot Boulevard and keep going until you reach Ankaboot Court. Drive down until you arrive at Hud Hud Gates," continued Zahra.

The children looked at each other in confusion. This was the strangest map they had ever read!

"Grandfather," said Zahra. "These street names sound so odd..."

"But also, a little familiar," added Yasser. "Where could we possibly have heard...?"

Before he could finish his sentence though, Grandfather was slowing down.

"Excellent map-reading, children! We are here already!" he said, as they pulled up in front of a pair of gigantic wrought-iron gates. The gates were made up of iron bars shaped into various animals and at the top, there was writing in Arabic script. Yasser was trying to make out what it said, when he noticed a beautiful, elegant, colourful bird standing just outside the gates to one side.

"Grandfather, look at that bird!" Yasser exclaimed.

"Has it escaped from the zoo?" Zahra asked in a whisper, leaning forward for a better look. She squealed as the bird suddenly spread its majestic wings and flew gracefully to the car, landing near Grandfather's window.

"Asalaamu Alaykum," the bird said, its voice gentle and melodious. "My name is Hud Hud. May I please see your entry pass?"

Yasser's jaw fell to the floor and for once, even Zahra was speechless!

"Did....did...did that bird just...talk?" Yasser stammered.

"And ask for a pass?" Zahra didn't know what was more astounding, that the bird could talk or what it had said!

Hud Hud turned its beady eyes on the two children and stared at them for a few seconds. Yasser could have sworn that it was trying very hard not to smile. *Don't be ridiculous, how can a bird smile?* he thought to himself and then remembered that he had just heard it speak as well.

The smile creeping across Grandfather's face however, was very real and very visible. Instead of reaching into his pocket to pay for a ticket, he turned back and asked Yasser to hand him the Holy Qur'an. He looked at the children as he took the sacred book carefully and softly whispered, "This is no ordinary book. Its pages are filled with Truth, Wisdom and a cure for every sickness. Even boredom!"

Yasser leaned over and whispered to Zahra, "This is going to be interesting."

When Hud Hud saw the Holy Qur'an, he closed his eyes, lowered his head and respectfully touched its cover with his beak. He stepped away from the car and made a sweeping motion with his wing. The gates immediately began to open slowly, revealing a misty swirl of blue-white light. The light began to pulsate and as it did, it pulled the car towards it in gentle, rocking movements. Yasser was hypnotised by the rhythm and closed his eyes as the car made one final forward move into the light's embrace.

When he opened his eyes, Yasser saw a huge sign in front of him that read:

WELCOME TO THE ANIMALS OF THE QUR'AN ZOO!

"*Ahlanwasahlan!* That's what it said in Arabic on the gate!" Yasser looked at Zahra and then back at Grandfather. This was no ordinary trip!

Grandfather chuckled in delight. "Yes, my dears, this is not your usual zoo! It's one filled with animals that are mentioned in the Holy Qur'an!"

"The street names!" Zahra exclaimed. "They sounded so familiar because they were the Arabic words for some of the animals we've read about in the Qur'an!" she continued. "Baqarah is cow, Naml is ant, Hoot is a whale…"

"And Hud Hud was the loyal bird that used to take special messages to and from Prophet Sulayman, peace be upon him," Yasser interrupted, straining against his seatbelt with excitement as they finally connected the dots in what had been a puzzling trip so far.

"You're both correct!" said Grandfather. "Well done! Now let's find a parking spot and begin exploring." Zahra and Yasser barely waited for the car to come to a stop before jumping out and rushing over to the huge zoo map that stood at the main entrance path.

Grandfather followed at a slower pace, pausing to pick up his Qur'an first. As the children scanned the map, they took turns to read out the list of animals on it: "Horses, camels, fish, dogs, donkeys, pigs, ants, cows..."

"Wow, there are over **THIRTY** animals here," said Yasser. "I didn't know there so many animals mentioned in the Qur'an. Where should we start?" he wondered out loud.

Grandfather opened his mouth to say something, but before he could, the Qur'an in his hand began to glow. It flung itself open to a page almost at its end. One of the verses on the page started giving out a soft glimmer, as if it had been highlighted with a golden pen. They all leaned in for a better look and Grandfather whispered, "Surah al-Ghashiyyah... verse seventeen."

"What does it say?" Zahra asked eagerly

Grandfather softly recited the Basmallah, as he did before beginning any recitation of the Qur'an, then he read the verse, first in Arabic, followed by the English translation.

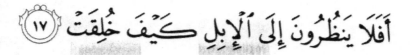

أَفَلَا يَنظُرُونَ إِلَى ٱلْإِبِلِ كَيْفَ خُلِقَتْ ﴿١٧﴾

"DO THEY NOT LOOK AT THE CAMELS? HOW WE CREATED THEM?"

"I think the Qur'an is guiding us to see the camels first!" Zahra said.

"I think you're right," replied Grandfather. He carefully shut the Qur'an, the glow fading away as the covers met again.

Zahra, Yasser and Grandfather checked the map for directions to the Camel Exhibition. "Let the adventure begin!" cried Yasser as he led the way - with Zahra following close on his heels - down the trail to the Eastern side of the zoo.

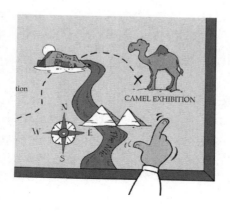

Chapter 3

As they went further down the path, it soon became a tree-lined avenue. Yasser looked over his shoulder and immediately stopped jogging. "We'd better wait for Grandfather," he said to Zahra, noticing that Grandfather was quite far behind them.

As they slowed down to a walking pace, they began to take notice of their environment. It was a bright day and the sun was a fiery, golden ball in the cloudless, baby blue sky above. The lush green trees that provided much needed shade cast a dappled shadow on the cobbled path. Zahra skipped from stone to stone, trying to step on the bright spots.

"Look, Yasser!" Zahra cried. "Berries!" She pointed to the plump deep-red berries sprinkled like confetti over the low bushes.

"You can eat them," Grandfather said. "Nothing here will harm you." He had finally caught up with them. "We are in a place that is protected by the Holy Qur'an."

Zahra smiled and quickly picked a few berries. "Yummy," she mumbled through a full mouth. "These are the sweetest berries I have ever tasted!"

"Alhamdulillah," Grandfather said, chuckling.

Yasser smiled and took Grandfather's right hand. Zahra licked her fingers and offered her sticky palm as well. Grandfather smiled and gave her his left hand. They skipped along, swinging arms and taking deep breaths of the sweet aroma that arose from the blanket of flowers at their feet.

"Sometimes the journey is just as beautiful as the destination," Zahra spoke her thoughts aloud. "I don't usually take the time to notice how pretty the world is."

Yasser nodded in agreement and then sighed. "Look all around us. Nature is so relaxing, so peaceful," he said taking a moment to breath in the fresh air.

Grandfather looked at both of them and smiled. "Yes, my dears, it's important to take time to look around us instead of rushing about being busy all the time."

"I always thought being bored was a bad thing," said Zahra, remembering how much she had complained that morning.

"Boredom sparks creativity and gives us a chance to reflect and open our eyes to the world around us," Grandfather said kindly.

"That's true," added Yasser. "We would never have thought of going on this adventure if we hadn't been bored!"

Jamal and Naaqa

CAMEL
EXHIBITION

Chapter 4

As Grandfather and the children walked on, the abundance of trees soon became sparse and the cobblestone path gave way to sand beneath their feet.

"Hey, where did all the flowers go?" Zahra asked looking back at the paradise they had left behind.

"Is it getting hot or is it just me?" Yasser asked, wiping beads of sweat from his forehead.

"I think we must be near the camel exhibition," Grandfather said smiling.

"Oh of course! Camels live in the desert!" Zahra remembered.

"Grandfather, when you recited the verse, there wasn't the word *jamal* in it," Yasser said, thoughtfully. "Isn't *jamal* the Arabic word for camel?"

"Ah yes, Yasser, well-spotted," said Grandfather. "The word in the verse was *ibil*. *Jamal* is another word for camel that is also used in the Qur'an. Although there is no surah named after a camel,

Allah often mentions the camel in the Qur'an using many of its different names."

"MORE THAN ONE NAME FOR A CAMEL?!" Zahra exclaimed.

Grandfather laughed, "Yes Zahra, there are about seven words for camel mentioned in the Qur'an, and dozens more in the Arabic language! They were a very common animal in Arabia, where Prophet Muhammad lived."

"Arabic is such an amazing language!" Yasser said, thinking that he'd love to master it someday.

Zahra began to imagine Arabia at the time of the Holy Prophet. "What was the name of Rasulullah's camel?" she asked, reflecting on how that camel must have felt to have the honour of carrying the most perfect human being on earth.

"His name was Qaswa," Grandfather replied with a smile, ready to tell a story. "When Prophet Muhammad arrived in Medina after the hijra, the people in Medina were so happy to see him, they all wanted to be his host and have him stay with them."

Yasser gasped, "imagine if Prophet Muhammad came to our house to stay, Zahra? Wouldn't that be amazing?"

A warm feeling rushed through Zahr'a body. What an exhilarating thought!

Grandfather continued as they trudged along, their feet sinking into the sand with every step. "The Holy Prophet did not want to offend anyone or hurt anyone's feelings by choosing one person to stay with over another, so he decided that the place his camel would stop would be where he would stay. And that is where they built the Prophet's house and his mosque!"

"Wow, imagine that!" Zahra exclaimed. "So Qaswa was inspired by Allah to stop on the spot that all Muslims visit today when they want to say salaam to the Prophet?"

"Yes!" agreed Grandfather. "We have always been told how kind the Holy Prophet was to all animals. He would stroke them with love, never overwork them and always tell his companions to do the same."

"HE TRULY IS THE BEST EXAMPLE IN EVERYTHING."

"Is Qaswa mentioned in the Holy Qur'an?" Yasser asked.

"No," replied Grandfather. "But look," he said pointing in the distance. "There are some camels approaching. They might be able to tell us stories about camels that *are* mentioned in the Qur'an!"

In a few minutes, two camels had ambled over and stood side-by-side towering above Grandfather and the children.

"Asalaamu alaykum!" said the larger camel. "We've been waiting for you. My name is Jamal, and this is my sister Naaqa."

"Delighted to meet you," Naaqa said, fluttering her thick eyelashes.

"Alaykum asalaam, we're glad to be here." Grandfather replied. The children hesitated before adding their replies. They were still getting used to talking to animals.

"Hop on! We're your rides and guides for this part of the exhibition." Jamal and Naaqa knelt down, bending their legs in a zig-zag fashion, so that Grandfather and the children could climb on. Yasser looked at Zahra. She could read his expression. Were they really going to ride camels? They looked at Grandfather who was already mounting Jamal without hesitation. Yasser shrugged his shoulders.

"Bismillah! Let's go!" he said, giving Zahra a hand as she clambered up onto Naaqa's saddle and then pulling himself up behind her.

"Lean back!" cried Naaqa to the children as she rose on her hind legs first. The children held on to the saddle handles and leaned back with all their might to stop from pitching forward. "Now to the front!" Naaqa lifted up her front legs and Yasser and Zahra followed her instructions, feeling the full force of gravity pulling against them.

"ALHAMDULILLAH!"

Finally, they were upright and the children relaxed, looking around from their new vantage point. "I can see so far into the distance!" said Zahra.

As the camels walked through the entrance of the exhibition, the children were able to appreciate just how high up they were. All around them the desert land stretched in every direction. Sand dunes lined the horizon and the only greenery to be seen were clumps of prickly cacti scattered sparsely around.

A hot breeze hit their faces and Zahra began to feel her skin prickle. "Are we going a long way, Naaqa?" she asked.

"Just to the next exhibition," Naaqa replied. "But we have plenty of stories to tell you along the way."

I hope we take a break somewhere to cool off, Zahra thought to herself, but as she looked around at the endless sea of sand on all sides, she wondered where that could possibly be?

Chapter 5

As they made their way, the camels matched their pace so they were walking side-by-side. Jamal looked over at the children who seemed uncomfortably hot. "It's actually not that a bad day for us," he said, smiling at their fragility. Sometimes, it gets to forty-three degrees. Very few animals can survive in the desert's extreme heat. We are the largest animals that live here and that's only possible because of the special features Allah has given us."

Zahra looked around the arid sandy planes. Jamal was right. There was no water in sight, no leafy trees for shade or to eat. How did the animals survive here?

"I hope one of those features is a built-in air conditioner?" Yasser asked. He couldn't help stroking Naaqa's soft fur. It was like wearing a blanket in the summer, he thought.

As if she read his thoughts, Naaqa replied, "The secret is in our fur. Because it is so thick, it helps us to keep the coolness we absorb inside our bodies. That way we can be cooler than the outside temperature. When it gets very cold in the winter, the fur works the other way around and keeps us warm!"

"Like one of those insulated bags that keep food warm or cold for longer?" Zahra said.

"Exactly like that," Grandfather agreed. "And their fur also prevents camels from sweating too much so they can keep more water in their bodies."

Naaqa gave Grandfather a nod of approval. "Yes, that's true, SubhanAllah!"

The mention of water made the children feel thirsty. "Asalaamu alayka ya Aba Abdillah," Zahra whispered. She couldn't imagine his thirst on the desert plains.

Yasser looked at Zahra sympathetically. Her lips were dry and she seemed sad. "Please Naaqa," he said out loud, "is there anywhere we can get some water? My sister is thirsty."

"Of course," Naaqa replied. "I could do with some water too. I haven't had anything to eat or drink for over a week."

"**A WEEK!**" Zahra exclaimed. "The longest I've gone without water is a few hours in the month of Ramadhan and that was super tough! How can you go without water for so long?"

"Allah has designed our bodies to allow us to use water in the best way possible," Jamal replied. "From the shape of our blood cells to our nostrils, every part of our body is designed to keep and use water without wasting even a drop."

Yasser and Zahra were amazed. "SubhanAllah!" they exclaimed, truly in awe of Allah's creation and design.

"Look! A pond!" Yasser pointed ahead to a shimmering pool surrounded by palm trees. It looked like a little heavenly garden in the middle of the barren desert. The camels trotted towards it quickly, aware that their passengers were thirstier than they were.

Chapter 6

The oasis was a peaceful haven in the middle of the desert. Some birds had gathered there to drink the cool, sweet water. *How many desert creatures must come here to quench their thirst?* thought Zahra. *How loving is Allah to create these places of hope and safety for them in this harsh desert! Why should I ever doubt that He would do the same for me in my life? When things are tough, I will remember that Allah is the Source of hope and safety for every creature,* she reminded herself.

Jamal and Naaqa lowered themselves so that Grandfather and the children could dismount.

"OOH! OOH! OUCH! HAAAA!" Zahra and Yasser hopped from one foot to the other as soon as they touched the ground.

"What's wrong?" Naaqa asked, concerned.

"The sand..." yelped Yasser. "It's so...hot!"

"How do you manage to sit on the burning sand like that, Jamal? If I stand here much longer my feet will turn into kebabs!" Zahra said.

Yasser couldn't wait for an answer. He threw his shoes off, peeled off his socks and ran into the water. "Aaaah, that feels sooooo good!"

Zahra laughed. Her brother could be so dramatic. "Sorry Jamal, were you saying something?"

"Yes," he said, smiling at Yasser's antics. "Our knees are covered with skin that is as hard and thick as horn. It's called callus and when we sit down, that's what protects us from the extreme heat of the sand." He had walked over to the pond while talking and now began to drink from it.

Grandfather looked at Yasser and Zahra. "Bismillah," he said, cocking his head to one side. They each bent down and picked up some cool water in their cupped hands. It felt like the sweetest drink they had ever tasted and left them feeling energised and filled with life again.

When they had drunk all that they could, Grandfather suggested they perform wudhu.

"Good idea!" said Yasser. "Wudhu always helps me cool down!"

As he splashed the cold water on his face and arms, Yasser reflected on how wudhu not only cooled down his body on a hot day, but whenever he became angry, frustrated or worried, it also helped him to calm down inside.

Grandfather, Yasser and Zahra stepped back and waited for the camels. They watched as Naaqa and Jamal continued gulping water in huge volumes.

"I know they're thirsty," Zahra whispered in Yasser's ear, "but how are they able to drink so much?" She patted her own swollen tummy in awe.

"Drinking water is a serious business for them," Grandfather said softly, not wanting to disturb the animals. "They can drink just over thirty gallons of water in one go."

"Does all that water stay in their humps?" Zahra asked.

"No, the humps are filled with fat," Grandfather said. "Their bodies use that fat as food, but if they don't get to water, then they can convert the fat into water as well."

Naaqa lifted her head from the shimmering pool and smacked her lips. "Alhamdulillah," she said and gave a happy sigh. She walked over to them as Jamal continued to drink for a little longer. "We can continue on our way as soon as Jamal has finished."

"Naaqa, you said you hadn't eaten for days as well. There's water in the oasis, but what do you eat that you can store away in your hump?" Zahra asked. All she had seen so far were thorny shrubs and cacti.

"Oh, we can eat whatever is around. Our rubbery lips make it easy for us to even eat thorns that are sharp enough to pierce leather!"

"**OUCH!**" Yasser winced as he tried to imagine eating thorns. "Doesn't that upset your tummy?" he asked

"Allah has provided for everything. We have a super-strong digestive system; we can eat pretty much anything!"

"SubhanAllah!" Zahra said.

Jamal lifted his head and burped loudly. He seemed more relaxed as well. "Come on, let us continue. We have some way left to go yet."

Chapter 7

As the camels paced along, Zahra thought she might fall asleep with the gentle, swaying motion of the ride. She was thinking about how peaceful and quiet the desert was when suddenly Naaqa stopped and raised her head higher. She looked at Jamal, who nodded back quickly.

"What's happening?" Yasser asked. No sooner had he uttered the question than they felt a strong gust of wind pull at their clothes.

"**SANDSTORM**," Jamal said with an urgent tone. "Quickly!" He motioned to Grandfather who reached into his pocket and pulled out his facemask and waved it in the air like a flag

"Yasser, Zahra! Put on your facemasks," instructed Grandfather, "and keep your eyes covered!"

Who would have thought these would have more than one use? Zahra wondered, doing as Grandfather said.

The wind picked up quickly and fiercely. Soon they could hear it howling as it approached in waves. Sand was flying everywhere. Zahra was glad to have Yasser behind her. She felt safer knowing her brother was with her and turned her face to bury it in his shirt. Yasser held on as well and she could feel him pressing his head down on her scarf to protect his eyes.

Naaqa and Jamal were running at a controlled speed, so although the ride was definitely bumpier, Grandfather and the children didn't feel as though they would fall off. After what felt like hours, but was probably just a few minutes, the howling began to ease and gradually silence returned.

"You can open your eyes and remove your masks now," said Jamal. "We've made it through the storm."

Yasser and Zahra were in shock. How was Jamal able to talk so calmly after what they had just walked through? How did he and Naaqa manage to see where they were going and breathe with all the sand in the air?

"Everyone okay?" asked Jamal.

"JazakAllah, we are! But, how did you do that?" Yasser asked. "I have sand in my hair and my throat feels itchy even though I was covered!"

"Me too," said Zahra. "My eyes are burning and it feels like the sand has got into my socks as well!"

"Alhamdulillah, all praise is for the Lord who gave us everything we need for the environment He placed us in," Naaqa said lovingly. "We have special nostrils that we can close almost completely so we don't need to breathe through them in a sandstorm."

"And I thought I could hold my breath for long because I can swim a length underwater!" said Yasser. "You guys are cool!"

"How could you see where you were going?" Zahra asked.

"Another adaptation and blessing. We have three sets of eyelids and two rows of thick eyelashes," explained Jamal. That's plenty of protection from sand grains. Besides, we had our eyes closed just like you, but one of those eyelids is transparent and so we can see any way!"

"Okay, correction," said Yasser, obviously impressed. "You're not jusr cool. You're super-cool!"

"Now I understand why the Qur'an asks us to reflect on how Allah made camels," Zahra said, remembering the verse in Surah al Ghashiyya.

Yasser propped his notebook against Zahra's back like they usually did when one of them wanted to write on the go. He quickly drew a camel and labelled all the special features that they had learnt about. He didn't want to miss out any of them later on.

Chapter 8

Zahra felt as though they had been transported back in time with the camel ride and vast expanses. It was so different from their busy highways and traffic jams at home. She began to imagine what life must have been like long ago, during the time of the prophets.

"What's that over there?" Yasser asked, excited. He was pointing to what looked like huge mountains that they were heading towards.

As they got closer, Zahra noticed beautiful houses carved expertly into the rock faces. "Wow!" she whispered. "These must have been built by some very clever people."

"They were rich too," added Grandfather

"Yes," Naaqa sighed, "these homes were made by the people of Thamud."

Zahra craned her neck to look carefully at the ruins that rose up over them like skyscrapers. There was something in the tone of Naaqa's voice and her sorrowful expression that made Zahra think that these people did not have a happy ending despite being wealthy and clever.

"Are they mentioned in the Qur'an?" Yasser asked.

"Yes," said Grandfather. "Twenty-three times."

"There must be a lot we can learn from them if they have been mentioned so many times!" Zahra said, thinking aloud.

"You're right." Naaqa nodded her head. "Their story includes a very special camel who was a sign from Allah."

"Oh Naaqa, please tell us about her!" Yasser pleaded.

Grandfather and the children dismounted from the camels so they could rest on the cool rocks at the foot of the mountains. Surrounded by these oddly beautiful ruins, they knew they were about to hear a story that would make them reflect in the way that only Qur'anic stories could.

Before the story began, Grandfather told the children that he wanted to share Imam Ali's advice that he had written in a letter in the form of a will to his son.

"What's a will?" Zahra asked.

"I think it's where someone writes down important things they want others to know and remember after they die." Yasser tried to explain.

"That's right," smiled Grandfather. "Here's the important advice Imam Ali gave:

SEE THE RUINED CITIES, THE DILAPIDATED PALACES, DECAYING SIGNS AND RELICS OF FALLEN EMPIRES OF PAST NATIONS.

THEN THINK ABOUT THE ACTIVITIES OF THOSE PEOPLE, WHAT THEY HAVE ALL DONE WHEN THEY WERE ALIVE AND WERE IN POWER, WHAT THEY ACHIEVED, WHERE, WHEN AND HOW THEY

WERE BROUGHT TO AN END, WHERE THEY ARE NOW; WHAT HAVE THEY ACTUALLY GAINED OUT OF LIFE AND WHAT WAS THEIR CONTRIBUTION TO HUMAN WELFARE.

"SubhanAllah! By coming to these ruins we are following the advice of Imam Ali!" Yasser exclaimed.

"Now I really can't wait to hear the story!" Zahra added.

They looked to Naaqa who had settled down and cleared her throat. She hesitated, as though the words were difficult to speak and then began in a sad voice, "Prophet Salih was an Arabian prophet sent to the people of Thamud. They liked him and wanted him to be a leader of their community. But when Prophet Salih began to preach about believing in one God, his people rejected his call. Instead, they turned their backs on Prophet Salih and continued to worship idols." Yasser could hear the sorrow growing in Naaqa's voice.

"One day, tired of Prophet Salih's advice, the people demanded a sign; a miracle from Allah to prove that he was telling the truth," Naaqa continued. "They thought if they made an impossible request, he would not be able to fulfil it and so they demanded that he produce a camel. But not just any camel! They wanted a female camel, who was pregnant and who could provide milk for all the people in the tribe. Best of all, they wanted this she-camel to emerge from the rocks and mountains!"

"Phew! That's a long list of demands!" Yasser exclaimed. "Although nothing is impossible for Allah," he quickly added.

Zahra was more sympathetic. "Maybe they just wanted to be a hundred percent sure that Prophet Salih was telling the truth. If he could perform this miracle, they would have to follow him without question, right?"

There was a silence following her statement and then Naaqa whispered, "One would hope so."

"So..." Yasser leaned forward eagerly. "Did Allah give the people of Thamud what they wanted? And then did they believe in Prophet Salih?"

"If only..." Naaqa said. She took a deep breath and began to recite from the Holy Qur'an. Jamal joined her and together they recited:

"O MY PEOPLE! THIS SHE-CAMEL OF ALLAH IS A SIGN FOR YOU. LET HER GRAZE FREELY IN ALLAH'S LAND, AND DO NOT CAUSE HER ANY HARM, FOR THEN YOU SHALL BE SEIZED BY A PROMPT PUNISHMENT."

"Yes," Naaqa said quietly. "Prophet Salih did call the pregnant she-camel to come forth from a large rock, just as the people of Thamud requested. It was a sign to prove his prophethood. But Allah set His rules as well. He commanded the people of Thamud to let the she-camel graze freely on the earth and to cause her no harm. They were also commanded to let her drink, and that the people would be able to milk her on a certain day."

Chapter 9

Yasser and Zahra waited with bated breath. *Would the people of Thamud fulfil the conditions that Allah had set?* The conditions sounded simple enough and Prophet Salih was there to guide them. Besides they now had proof that he really was a prophet. But Naaqa still looked grieved. She opened her mouth to speak, but a sad, bleating cry came out that echoed through the ruins around them.

"Oh Naaqa!" Zahra stroked her neck. "Did they chase away the she-camel instead of looking after her?"

At this, full tears fell from Naaqa's deep black eyes, until Jamal finally said. "The people of Thamud killed the she-camel."

Yasser and Zahra gasped.

"How could they do that?" Zahra exclaimed. "*Why* would they do that?" She was in shock. She continued to gently stroke Naaqa in an attempt to soothe her. Allah had created such wonderful animals and mentioned them in the Qur'an because He wanted human beings to love and learn from them. The she-camel had been a gift from Allah to the people of Thamud as a sign from Him. Why would they treat her in this horrible way?

Jamal finished the story, because Naaqa couldn't. "The worst thing was that when Prophet Salih warned them that Allah was angry with them and they should repent, the people of Thamud laughed and asked him to bring on Allah's punishment if he was truthful."

"How could they doubt his truth after everything he did?" asked Yasser. "Such foolish people!"

"After three days there was an earthquake accompanied by a terrible, loud sound and the people of Thamud were all destroyed except Prophet Salih and the few companions who had believed and followed him."

There was silence for a few minutes as the group seemed to be lost in their own thoughts. Zahra looked around again, still captivated by the beauty of the houses carved so expertly into the mountains. *Allah has preserved the ruins here for a reason,* she thought, *perhaps as a reminder to everyone.*

Yasser followed Zahra's gaze, then crinkled his nose, "How could people who were so clever make such an awful mistake? How could they think that they were stronger than Allah?"

"All this power," Grandfather made a sweeping motion with his arm, "made them forget that they needed Allah." He sighed.

"When I do things well, it's hard not to feel proud of myself," Yasser confessed, a little embarrassed.

Zahra thought of the things she had been proud of, from her beautiful clothes to her grades at school.

"There is nothing wrong with being pleased when you have nice things or when you have worked hard and achieved good results." Grandfather put his arms around Yasser and Zahra. "But we should always remember that it is Allah who granted us those gifts and helped us to achieve our aims. Without His help and guidance, we would not have anything. All praise and all thanks are for Him."

"The more I have, the more I need to thank Allah," Zahra added.

"Yes," agreed Grandfather. "Wealth should not make you proud, arrogant or neglectful of Allah."

Yasser felt his heart absorb his grandfather's words deeply. The reminders he gave were like medicine for him. *Next time I feel proud or think I am better than others, I will remember that everything I have is from Allah, and all praise and all thanks are for Him*, he silently promised himself.

Grandfather thanked Allah for his wonderful grandchildren. They had open hearts, always willing to learn and improve. *That* is the most important thing, Grandfather thought.

Chapter 10

Yasser and Zahra continued talking to Jamal and Naaqa as they sat amongst the ruins. They had quickly realised what wise and wonderful creatures the camels were and wanted to learn as much as they could about them. As they chatted and shared the snacks they had brought, they discussed the people of Thamud and what they could learn from the story. By the time they had finished their picnic, the children had managed to note down ten lessons they had learnt from the people of Thamud and the story of the she-camel

TOP TEN LESSONS WE CAN LEARN FROM THE PEOPLE OF THAMUD

1. Always thank Allah for the things you have and realise they are from Him.

2. Make a good first impression. Prophet Salih was wise, good and respectful before he started preaching. (Just like Prophet Muhammad!)

3. Don't follow the mistakes of your ancestors. The people of Thamud wanted to worship idols because their ancestors did in the past, even if they secretly knew it was wrong.

4. Allah can do anything. When the people told Prophet Salih to ask Allah to make a she-camel out of a rock, Allah could easily do this.

5. Arrogance can make a person blind to the truth. Some of the people knew that this camel was from Allah, but because of their pride, they remained in denial.

6. Miracles of Allah should be respected!

7. You should be kind to animals, they are creations of Allah.

8. Your wealth cannot save you from a punishment. The people of Thamud were certain that their stone houses could save them from Allah's punishment, but they were wrong.

9. Allah is All Merciful. Prophet Salih told his people to repent as Allah was willing to forgive them, but they were too stubborn.

10. Allah always provides guidance. It is up to us to follow it.

Jamal looked at the sun. "We've been here for an hour!" he said in surprise.

"Time flies when you're having fun," Zahra laughed.

"We'd better get you to the next exhibition," Naaqa said. "It's not far from here."

"What are we going to see next?" Yasser asked.

Just then, as if in answer to Yasser's question, the Qur'an let out a ray of light. It shone and shimmered and then opened by itself again.

"SubhanAllah!" Yasser and Zahra exclaimed, wide-eyed. The page before them was from Surah Ara'f.

"What does the verse say?" Zahra asked, squinting at the words.

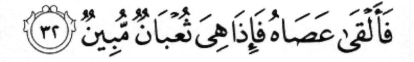

فَأَلْقَىٰ عَصَاهُ فَإِذَا هِىَ ثُعْبَانٌ مُّبِينٌ ﴿٣٢﴾

"SO MOSES THREW HIS STAFF, AND SUDDENLY IT WAS A SNAKE, MANIFEST."

"A SNAKE?" Zahra repeated.

Jamal and Naaqa nodded, amused by Zahra's reaction.

"I guess that means we're going to the snakes next!" Yasser beamed.

Grandfather, Yasser and Zahra expertly mounted the camels and they galloped through the desert, as fast as horses until they arrived at a huge archway. Above it there was a sign: "Snake Exhibition".

"We have to leave you here," Jamal said. "We really enjoyed the time we spent with you and we'll remember you always."

Yasser and Zahra hugged the camels and thanked them for everything. They were so grateful to have learnt so much from them. What could the next exhibition possibly have in store for them?

thu'baan

Chapter II

"I'm looking forward to meeting a snake," Yasser said. "They seem like such mysterious creatures."

"I'm glad you think ssssso!"

Yasser and Zahra turned around to see where the voice had come from, but they couldn't see anyone.

"Down here!"

Yasser and Zahra's looked down and there, just inches from their feet was a majestic creature coiled on the desert sand.

"Assssssssssssalaamu alaykum," hissed the snake.

"Wa alykum asalaam wa rahmatullah, may Allah's peace and blessing be with you," Grandfather replied reverently.

The grassy green snake looked as though he was covered in ruby red jewels. He glided smoothly across the sand and came closer to the children. His scaly skin glistened in the sunlight and his movements were completely mesmerising. He looked deep into the children's eyes with a hypnotising stare. Then he broke into a wide smile that showed his fangs. He looked scary, but the children knew nothing in this zoo would harm them, so they felt safe, especially because Grandfather was standing right next to them.

The serpent raised his head. "My name isssssss Thu'baan," he announced in a grand voice. "I am here to take you on a mosssst magical adventure. Welcome to Egypt!"

"Thooban?" Zahra repeated, trying to pronounce correctly.

"Thu'baan" the snake corrected. "Thu' and then baan." He glided quickly in the sand leaving an imprint in the sand that spelled out his name in Arabic.

It was easier to read his name in Arabic than English, because they could now see the letter 'ayn' and the sukoon that couldn't be described in English.

ثُعْبان

Zahra had been learning how to pronounce a sukoon in her Qur'an lessons, so she gave it a second try. "Thu'baan...Thu'baan. Nice to meet you Thu'baan!" Zahra said, pleased that she had mastered the pronunciation.

Thu'baan nodded. "Perfect. Now, follow me as quick as you can."

Thu'baan slithered along, stopping every few minutes because he was so much faster than Grandfather and the children. He led them along the River Nile, allowing them to stop to quench their thirst and enjoy the warm breeze through the rustling river reeds.

Yasser had been watching Thu'baan and didn't know what to make of him. Snakes seemed so mysterious; quiet and cunning, clever yet beastly. He wasn't sure whether to be terrified or in awe of this creature. After a while, he decided to speak up.

"Thu'baan, please could you tell us a little bit about yourself?" he asked, pulling out his notebook. "I'd like to write down what we learn."

"Of coursssse," replied Thu'baan. "Let'ssss ssseeee...I can sssmell with my tongue, I can ssssee heat, my venom can kill and cure, I hear with my jaw and I can crawl out of my ssssskin."

Yasser dropped his pen and put his notepad down. "Whhhaaaat?" he exclaimed, with his eyebrows raised. "I...I...you can... I mean..." he stuttered, until he finally conceded and could only utter the words: "SubhanAllah."

They all laughed heartily. Thu'baan continued to talk to the children, explaining his cryptic statements to them, whilst they scribbled rapidly into their notebooks.

Some snakes can't see well and use other senses to find prey. They have openings called pit holes in front of their eyes which can sense heat given off by warm-blooded prey.

Snakes flick their long, tongues to pick up chemical molecules from the air. The tongue carries the smelly molecules back to the roof of the snake's mouth where they're analysed!

Snakes don't have ears to hear sound waves in the air. Instead, bones in their lower jaw pick up vibrations in the ground or water.

Chapter 12

"Follow me! This way!" Thu'baan called out as he slithered ahead of them. He was so fast, even without legs! He seemed to simply glide on the surface of the sand. They had left the banks of the river and turned to go inland. Thu'baan had led them straight to a small cluster of pyramids and they were now almost running to keep up with him as he headed to the foot of the closest one.

He slid through a small open door that seemed to appear out of nowhere in the wall of the pyramid. The doorway was just a dark hole made of missing stones at the base of the triangular structure. Yasser and Zahra quickly followed their guide in, afraid they might lose sight of him.

It was a relief to be out of the sun, the coolness of the pyramid was calming and within seconds, their eyes began to acclimatise to the darkness. They could make out the dim outlines of the chamber they had entered. It was large and had a high ceiling, giving a feeling of openness and space.

"Make yourselves comfortable," Thu'baan directed the children. Grandfather entered the room and collapsed on the floor next to Yasser and Zahra. He was grateful for the rest too.

Now Thu'baan had centre-stage and the children could tell he was loving the attention.

"TODAY I WILL TAKE YOU ON A MOST MAGICAL ADVENTURE! I PRESENT TO YOU, EGYPT AT THE TIME OF PROPHET MUSA!"

All of a sudden, one of the dark walls of the pyramid came alive with rows of animated images depicting Egypt's past. Giant golden pyramids and huge temples with daunting statues appeared in front of them.

"AWESOME!" Zahra exclaimed, her voice echoing in the pyramid.

"They look like hieroglyphics!" Yasser added in excitement, remembering his history lessons about the way ancient Egyptians had carved symbols to write and tell stories.

Zahra pointed to the image closest to her. "Who are all these people building the temples?" she asked. "They look so poor and exhausted."

Yasser looked at the worn-out men closely. They were working in the midday heat, with the blazing sun drawn low above their heads. Officers in gold and crimson robes threatened them with whips as they carried heavy boulders and chiselled into the rock. Even though it was just an image, the fear in their posture was evident. These men were truly oppressed.

"They are the Bani Israel," replied Thu'baan. "The descendants of Prophet Yaqub. They came to Egypt at the time of Prophet Yusuf, and over the years were enslaved by the evil king Firawn. He used them as slaves to build his temples and treated them very poorly.

Yasser frowned. He could feel the heat of anger rise in his body. The injustice of what had been done was unbearable. "Where is Firawn?" he asked, inspecting the pyramid walls.

"This looks like a palace!" Zahra said, pulling Yasser towards her and pointing to another image. The building in this drawing had high stone walls embellished with paintings and encrusted with polished jewels.

"Look through that window over there," Thu'baan instructed.

Yasser and Zahra leaned in to get a closer look at the scene. Inside were two men who looked like brothers. They were dressed in simple clothes; each wore a long shirt, worn-out robes and sandals. One of them was holding what looked like some kind of walking stick.

The third man in the room, standing opposite them, looked completely different. His crisp white robe was belted with solid gold and his headdress was so grand it made his head look ten times bigger than anyone else's. Thick black eye-liner framed his eyes which gave him a menacing expression. Zahra could not stand to look at him for long. She shuddered, but the two men did not seem frightened. They stood calmly in the room.

Thu'baan rattled his tail in what seemed to be a cue to begin a spectacular animation. The images started to move! One of the brothers stepped forward towards the angry king. He spoke calmly and gently. "We are the messengers of the Lord of the World. You need to let the Bani Israel go so we can lead them to a new land. Let us guide you to your Lord so that you will be in awe of Him."

Zahra and Yasser looked at Grandfather in shock. "Is that Prophet Musa?" Zahra asked slowly.

Grandfather nodded

"And is that Firawn?" Yasser said, feeling the same anger he had when he saw the drawings of the slaves.

Grandfather confirmed that it was.

"Yassser! Zahra! Do you know who the third man isss?" Thu'baan asked.

The children looked back the drawing. He had the same humble expression as Prophet Musa, and his face glowed with the light of faith. "Could it be Prophet Musa's brother?" Zahra wondered.

"Yesssss!" exclaimed Thu'baan. "That is Prophet Haroon. He supported his brother's mission."

"Look at the way they are speaking to Firawn," Yasser said. "I'm so angry with Firawn for all the oppression he caused, but Prophet Musa is talking to him like you would to a friend. How does he control his speech like that?"

"Allah ordered Prophet Musa to speak to Firawn with gentle words," said Grandfather. "Allah was giving Firawn a chance to be guided and to do the right thing by freeing the Bani Israel."

"Wow!" Zahra said, looking away. "Is this how merciful Allah is? He still wants to guide even those who have gone so far astray? Allah is always kind, patient and peaceful. We've seen what Firawn is like and we know the story of how he killed the baby boys of the Bani Israel. He is completely evil, yet Allah is giving him a chance."

Zahra felt her eyes water as she thought about Allah's mercy. How many times had she refused to forgive or fought with her friends over the smallest misunderstandings? Yet she had always relied on the mercy of Allah to help her in all situations. Now she was beginning to understand the true extent of Allah's mercy. *He is not a God who is angry or looks for faults in others so He can punish them,* she thought. *He is all-Merciful, so kind and so, so loving.* Her eyebrows furrowed as she delved deeper into her own realisation. She promised herself that she would try to be more sympathetic and kinder to others instead of looking for faults.

Suddenly the Firawn-drawing thumped his fist on his throne and Zahra was shaken out of her thoughts. "You expect me to listen to you?" he bellowed "What is the Lord of the Worlds you speak of?"

Prophet Musa replied confidently: **"HE IS THE SUSTAINER OF THE HEAVENS AND THE EARTH, IF YOU HAVE DEEP FAITH."**

Thu'baan let out a long, frustrated hiss. "At the time of Firawn, people did not think that Allah was their Lord and Sustainer. Instead, they thought that every generation and every place had their own lord and Firawn had claimed that he was the lord and sustainer of Egypt."

"Now I can see why he's so angry," said Yasser. "Believing in Prophet Musa would mean giving up a lot of power."

"That's true," said Grandfather. "The idea that Allah is the Only Lord of the Worlds is at the centre of tawhid - the belief that Allah is one."

"Of course!" exclaimed Yasser. "We say it every day in Surah Fatiha, 'Allah is Rabbul Alameen'."

Suddenly the room echoed with Firawn's laughter. "**HAHAHAHA**! Are you saying that the Lord of the Heaven and the Earth is the same? What nonsense!"

Prophet Musa waited and then spoke clearly with confidence. "Yes, I am. He is your Lord and the Lord of the previous generations."

Firawn's face fell and he choked midway on his laughter. He stood up and walked towards Prophet Musa and Prophet Haroon. His expression was sinister and he raised his fist threateningly at the brothers. "If you dare say there is a lord beside me, I will put you in prison!"

"Oh no!" Zahra cried, looking at Thu'baan. "What will Prophet Musa do?"

Thu'baan smiled, revealing his friendly fangs. "Sounds like it's time for a snake to make an appearance!"

"A snake?" Yasser looked curious.

"Watch!" Thu'baan said, indicating to the pyramid wall with his eyes.

Prophet Musa stepped forward, unafraid. "What if I have a sign?" he calmly replied.

"What sign?" bellowed Firawn.

Prophet Musa threw down his staff and as it hit the palace floor it turned into a snake! Then he put his hand into his chest and when he removed it, it shone like a blinding beam of light.

Yasser and Zahra could not believe what they were seeing. "How did he do that?" asked Yasser.

"Firawn was wondering the same thing," said Thu'baan. "He knew a lot about magic, but he had not seen anything like this before."

Chapter 13

The images had stopped moving and a silence had fallen once again in the darkened chamber. Yasser traced the frozen images on the wall with his finger. He let his hand follow the path of Prophet Musa and Prophet Haroon out of the palace. He was still surprised that Firawn had let them go. Further along, he saw images of ministers and magicians rushing towards the palace. *I guess Firawn will need a plan to defeat Prophet Musa,* Yasser thought. He felt strangely calm compared to his initial anger at the evil ruler.

Zahra's excitement interrupted his musings. "Thu'baan, what happened next? Did Firawn accept Prophet Musa's claim? Why are there so many ministers and magicians entering the palace?"

"Firawn called for the best magicians from every corner of his kingdom. He offered them great rewards to display their best magic and defeat Prophet Musa," Thu'baan said. He pointed with his tail to the second wall of the pyramid and immediately, it lit up with colourful images of a festival. Thousands of people were gathered in what seemed to be the town square and the murmur of the crowds filled all corners of the room.

Yasser leaned in closely. "Look there Zahra, I think the magicians are arguing with each other."

The images began to move once again and this time it was the magicians who spoke.

"Confronting Musa like this is not a good idea!" exclaimed one magician in frustration.

"He is not an ordinary man," said another.

"He's definitely not a magician," protested a third.

Firawn seemed to sense their reluctance, but he was stubborn and arrogant. **"I AM THE LORD OF EGYPT AND YOU SHALL DO AS I SAY!"** he ordered. "If you defeat him, I will make you my close ones and give you all the rewards you want!" Firawn added, hoping the bribe would persuade them.

He pushed the magicians forward and they stood to their full height in front of the cheering crowd. They puffed out their chests in an attempt to appear confident, though the fear in their eyes betrayed them as they stood in front of Prophet Musa, a clear man of God.

The magicians summoned the attention of the crowd and everyone fell silent. Prophet Musa gestured gracefully, allowing the magicians to lead the proceedings.

The first magician nodded, accepting the challenge. A ripple ran through the drawings, indicating the excitement of the people. "In the name of Firawn, lord of Egypt!" he roared.

Colourful smoke rose from the pyramid floor. Yasser, Zahra and Grandfather tried to see through it at the images on the wall, but they could barely make out what was happening. It seemed that the magicians were throwing potions on the ground and creating clouds of dust that obstructed everyone's view. As the dust settled, there was a collective gasp as the ground in front of the magicians was covered in large, terrifying snakes. With mouths wide open showing fangs ready to attack, they writhed across the square, hissing furiously.

Zahra felt a pang of worry. She looked across the wall to try and see the rest of the scene. How would Prophet Musa be able to defeat them? Their display was so impressive.

"Watch," Grandfather reassured her, smiling in anticipation.

After calmly taking in the scene for a few seconds, Prophet Musa stepped forward, said 'Bismillahir Rahmanir Raheem' and threw down his staff. It immediately turned into a serpent, far bigger and more powerful than the rest! Prophet Musa's staff-serpent flattened its neck in attack-mode, lunged forward and gobbled up the rest of the snakes as if they were a bowl of spaghetti!

The crowd, the magicians and Firawn all looked on in shock. There was an endless moment of deafening silence and then the magicians collapsed to the floor in prostration. **"WE BELIEVE IN YOUR GOD!"** they declared to Prophet Musa in front of the entire gathering. **"WE BELIEVE IN YOUR LORD!"**

Yasser and Zahra gasped and turned around to look at Thu'baan who was swaying and smiling proudly. The magicians had recognised the truth and humbled themselves before it. What a difference from the people of Thamud!

Yasser's eyes shone brightly. He felt an energy rush through his body. "Yes!" he punched his fist in the air. Prophet Musa had been successful! And the magicians - what amazing men they had been! Yasser hoped he would be able to follow the truth whenever he found it. He imagined the return of Imam Mahdi (AJTF).

The people in Egypt understood magic and so when Prophet Musa performed a miracle better than any magic, they recognized straight away that it was from Allah. When Prophet Muhammad spoke to the Arabs who loved poetry, they quickly realised that the Qur'an was far superior than any poetry a human could compose and submitted to the truth of his message. What would Imam Mahdi do to convince people of his mission? *How will he prove to the world that he is the true Imam?* Yasser wondered. Yasser sincerely prayed that he would be with the twelfth Imam to see that miracle and that he would have the humility to accept it.

The beautiful moment did not last long. A loud cry interrupted Yasser's thought. He turned to the third and final wall of the pyramid that had now come to life.

"HOW DARE YOU?" snarled Firawn, pointing his bejewelled finger at the magicians in accusation **"HOW DARE YOU BELIEVE WITHOUT MY PERMISSION?"**

"Arrest these traitors!" he ordered his guards. The crowd gasped as the soldiers surrounded the magicians who continued to praise Allah. "You will regret this!" threatened Firawn. "I promise you, you will regret that you ever saw this day!" And as they were carried away, Firawn pronounced a most painful punishment for them: he ordered that their hands and feet be cut off and that they should be crucified! But even this threat did not deter the magicians. They stood firm in their faith in Prophet Musa and his Lord.

"DO WHATEVER YOU WANT!" one magician boldly stated. "Your punishments can only harm us in this life. We now believe in our Lord, we hope He will forgive our sins and forgive us for what you forced us to do."

Zahra clapped her hand across her mouth. What

a scene! These were people who had not believed in Allah. In fact, the magicians were sinners, as magic is a great sin and their lifestyle had been the complete opposite of what Allah loved. Yet now, they were holding so firmly to their faith in God, no matter how much Firawn threatened them. *How was this possible?* Zahra wondered.

"SubhanAllah," Zahra finally said as the wall quietened. "No matter what we have done in our lives, Allah always tries to guide us back to Him."

"If we go back to Allah, he will completely forgive us for everything we have done in our past," Yasser added hopefully.

"You're right, children," agreed Grandfather. "We must keep our hearts humble and open to Allah's guidance all around us."

The pyramid had become quiet and dark again. Thu'baan, Grandfather, Yasser and Zahra sat together, using the time to reflect on everything they had witnessed.

"Thu'baan," Yasser finally said. "Is *that* the difference between the magicians and Firawn? That the magicians kept an open heart and Firawn did not, because he was arrogant?"

"Yesss, I'm afraid that wasss the case and it wasss what led to his downfall," said Thu'baan.

Thu'baan was pleased to see that the children had understood the lessons of this great miracle.

He led them out of the pyramid and into the open sky. Yasser quickly covered his eyes with the back of his hand, and Zahra pulled her scarf over her face. They blinked away the flashes of light that temporarily blinded their vision until their eyes became accustomed to the sunlight again.

"I mussst take my leave now," Thu'baan said. "Keep following the path of the Nile! The story of Prophet Musa is far from over and there are still lots more animals to see!"

Chapter 14

Grandfather, Yasser and Zahra continued to walk along the path of the River Nile. Yasser kept wondering what happened to Prophet Musa after the miracle with the snake. Did Firawn give up and let Prophet Musa take Bani Israel out of Egypt?

"I don't think that Firawn would let Prophet Musa lead the Bani Israeel away without more of a fight," he said out loud as they walked.

"You're right. Years passed by after what we just saw," Grandfather said. "The people who followed Prophet Musa went through difficult times. Firawn threatened them and punished them in the worst ways possible. Allah was testing them, but sadly, even Prophet Musa's own people went against him. They began to doubt whether he would lead them out of Egypt after all."

"What happened then?" Zahra asked, curious to know how Prophet Musa dealt with this rebellion from both his enemies and his followers.

"Allah sent signs to the people of Firawn," Grandfather replied.

"What kind of signs? More miracles?"

The Holy Qur'an began to shine as if in answer to Zahra's question. Grandfather gently took the Holy Book from his pocket, kissed it gently and handed it to Zahra. She was surprised, but she reached out to take it from Grandfather. Immediately, the Qur'an opened to Surah al-Araf, verse, 133.

"What does it say?" asked Yasser.

Zahra remembered that she was in wudhu, so she placed her finger over the verse and began to recite. Although the verse was in Arabic, she found that she could understand its meaning!

"It says:

SO WE SENT UPON THEM THE STORM AND LOCUSTS AND LICE AND FROGS AND BLOOD, AS SIGNS DISTINCT FROM EACH OTHER. YET THEY SHOWED ARROGANCE, AND THEY WERE A GUILTY PEOPLE."

"More animals mentioned in the Qur'an," said Yasser, his excitement muted when he heard the list. "Are we going to see the locusts, lice and frogs next?" he asked in trepidation.

"Not today, Yasser." Grandfather replied.

Zahra looked up from the Qur'an in the dread. She and Yasser turned their eyes to the Nile and imagined how it would look with dark red waters and drooping reeds withering away along its banks.

"There was a famine and reduced harvest. Then a few years later, the water in the Nile turned to blood. When the people didn't learn from all that, Allah finally sent the insects and swarms of locusts, lice and frogs," Grandfather said with a solemn face.

Zahra was confused. "I thought signs were always good things that were supposed to lead you to Allah."

"Zahra, my dearest, Allah sent these misfortunes to guide the people to Him, to help them remember Him. Anything that reminds us of Allah is a sign from Him because it is pointing us in the right direction."

"This reminds me of coronavirus," Yasser said.

"So many people are suffering and it seems like a curse or a punishment of some sort, but what if we could learn from it and use it as an opportunity to get closer to Allah?"

"Coronavirus? A way to get closer to Allah?" Zahra asked.

"Yeah...." Yasser nodded.

"I see what you mean. We could look at it as a way of Allah calling us, reminding us that He is the most powerful and we need to turn back to Him."

Grandfather looked from Yasser to Zahra. "You're very right," he said. "Everything that happens in our lives is an opportunity to get closer to Allah. It's easy to be thankful to Him in times of happiness and remember that everything comes from Him. We also need to return to Him in times of sadness and uncertainty, knowing that He is our only protector and hope for help."

Nahla

Chapter 15

"Hmm, let's see," said Grandfather, looking at the map as if he was testing the children. "Where should we go next?"

"Grandfather, we need to look in the Qur'an for guidance," Yasser reminded him.

"Ah yes, of course!" Grandfather replied, smiling. He took out his Qur'an and gave it to Yasser. "Here. You ask this time."

Yasser took the Qur'an from Grandfather with both hands and touched it to his forehead out of respect, just as his Qur'an teacher did before class. Then he kissed it and whispered a prayer for guidance.

Although he had seen the Qur'an hum and glow in Grandfather's hands, when the Holy Book began to do the same in his hands, he felt a shiver run down his spine. The Qur'an was talking to him! Allah was talking to him! Excitement and awe washed over him.

Then the cover of the Qur'an lifted up slowly and the pages ruffled, causing a gentle breeze to blow onto Yasser's face. He took a deep breath and he smelt a perfume like none other. When the ruffling stopped, the pages remained open to one spread of verses. They all looked at the surah.

"It's the sixteenth surah! Surah Nahl," Yasser cried.

"The honey bee!" Zahra said at the same time and they both giggled.

Grandfather opened the map to find the directions to the Bee Exhibition. It wasn't far but they needed to change direction and head north.

As they began to walk, the air cooled, and soon after, when they climbed to the top of a small sand dune, they could see the familiar archway that was the entrance to a new exhibition below them at the foot of the hill.

The children laughed and ran, sliding and slipping, towards the doorway. As soon as they reached the entrance of the exhibition, they gasped in wonder. While behind them lay vast desert sands, through the arch, they could see a completely different scene.

A carpet of lush green grass spread out in front of them. There was the gurgling sound of a stream running somewhere and countless flowers of every shape and colour filled the land. They had never seen such a beautiful sight!

"SubhanAllah!" Zahra could find no other words to describe how she was feeling.

"BLESSED BE YOUR SUSTAINER'S NAME FULL OF MAJESTY AND BOUNTY!" Grandfather recited the verse from Surah Rahman. He too was overcome by the beauty that was before them.

"What did you say?" Yasser asked Grandfather.

Grandfather smiled, he loved Yasser's curious nature and how he was always keen to learn more. **"DHUL JALAALI WAL IKRAAM** is one of Allah's names. It means that Allah is the Lord of Majesty and Bounty. Allah is mighty and majestic and powerful, but He is also gentle, bountiful and beautiful. Allah is in perfect balance and loves us to be in balance too."

"That's amazing," Yasser responded as he observed the complete harmony and balance around him.

Chapter 16

"BUZZZZZZZZZZZZZZZZZZZZZ."

Yasser and Zahra jumped in surprise as they saw something fly towards them.

"Could this beeee our guide?" Yasser asked, unable to control his giggles. "Maybeeeeeee," he answered his own question and broke out into a hearty laugh. He knew a host of bee jokes.

Grandfather chuckled and Zahra tried to roll her eyes, but ended up laughing too. She could not resist her brother's jokes. It wasn't that she found them funny, in fact, sometimes she had no idea what he was giggling about, but his laugh was so full of life that it filled a room and made anyone who heard it laugh along with him.

"Asalaamu alaykum! I'm Nahla, the honey bee!" the little brown and yellow insect announced, flying around her guests. "I'm so pleased to see you!"

"Alaykum asalaam," Yasser and Zahra replied. They had a feeling this would be a lot of fun. "We're pleased to meet you too, though we can hardly see your face!"

"Oh, we'll fix that in a second," Nahla said, nodding at Grandfather.

"Bismillah," Grandfather winked.

Zahra and Yasser were watching Nahla curiously as she began to buzz from flower to flower when suddenly they began to feel a strange tingle in their hands and feet.

"Grandfather...? Something very strange is happening" Zahra looked at him, puzzled.

"Why is everything growing taller so fast?" Yasser shouted as the trees and bushes around them began to shoot up above their heads.

"They're not growing taller," Zahra cried out. "WE'RE...SHRINKING!"

There was a final pop and a jolt and then all three of them were standing on the ground, surrounded by huge rocky boulders and blades of grass that towered over their heads.

"Ya Dhal Jalaali wal Ikram!" Yasser exclaimed. "Amazing! Truly Allah's Majesty knows no bounds!" They looked around, taking in their new perspective.

"See how different things look from down here. It's like a different world altogether," Zahra observed.

There was a roaring buzzing sound like that of a dozen helicopters hovering over them and they saw a huge, monstrous creature flying down to them.

"Grandfather!" Yasser and Zahra took shelter behind him.

"Don't worry, children, it's just our guide, Nahla!"

The children looked out in wonder and finally saw how different the honey bee looked when they were so tiny. Her body and legs were covered with hair, so she looked almost furry. With her large eyes and slowly swinging antennae, she had a strong, wise look about her.

"Come on, you lot," she said. "Hop on! We bees are bizzzzzy creatures. We don't have time to waste! We have a hive to explore."

Yasser and Zahra looked at each other in delight. They were going to see a real hive and go inside it! They climbed up onto Nahla's back, with Grandfather sitting between the children. Each of them grabbed on to clumps of Nahla's hair as she hovered and then took off at high speed.

"WHEEEEEEEE!" Zahra screamed. The ride was like a roller-coaster, weaving between giant flowers and leaves, the wind rushing past their ears.

"I can't beeeeelieve we're flying on a bee!" Yasser yelled, not wanting to lose the chance to slip in a joke.

Chapter 17

"Our hive is ahead, in that willow tree," said Nahla as they flew.

Despite the rapid ride, Grandfather had remained calm. He couldn't quite reach his Qur'an, so he recited verse sixty-eight of Surah Nahl from memory:

"AND YOUR LORD INSPIRED THE BEE SAYING: 'MAKE YOUR HOME IN THE MOUNTAINS, AND ON THE TREES AND IN WHAT THEY BUILD',"

"That's from the surah in the Qur'an named after us!" buzzed Nahla in delight.

How did Allah inspire a bee? wondered Yasser, saving the question at the back of his mind to ask Grandfather later.

Zahra, on the other hand, was thinking of the people of Thamud again. *They became proud because they thought they were clever for building homes in mountains. But tiny little bees can do it too!*

Yasser and Zahra were jolted out of their thoughts by the sudden roar of buzzing that surrounded them. They looked ahead and saw that Nahla was heading straight for a wall of busy, buzzing bees!

"Watch out!" shouted Yasser.

"**AAAAAAAAH!**" cried Zahra.

But Nahla simply and smoothly wove in and out between the bees in spaces only she seemed able to see. The children closed their eyes and waited for the ride to end. Finally, Nahla settled in one place and they were able to look up and take in their surroundings.

They had landed on the edge of the hive and while there were dozens of bees swarming in and out of it, they seemed to be in safe from the activity.

"You'll need to break off a bit of this," Nahla pointed with one of her legs to a large lump. "Take a little bit and put it in your ears to help with the sound when we go inside."

Grandfather, Yasser and Zahra did as they were told. The lump felt soft and malleable to touch, a bit like warm candle wax.

"It's a special beeswax," Nahla said, "made for our zoo. When you put a ball of it in your ear, it'll block out all the buzzing and you will only be able to hear my voice."

"Ooooh!" Yasser was the first to try it out. The moment he put the second ball of wax into his ear, the loud buzzing faded away into the background. He looked at Nahla and gave her a thumbs-up.

"Is it working?" Nahla asked. Her voice coming through crystal clear.

"Beee-oootifully!" Yasser said, with a wide smile.

Once they all had their special ear-plugs in place, they climbed back up onto Nahla and flew into one of hexagonal holes of the hive.

Chapter 18

There were thousands of bees inside, all working hard, buzzing in different directions. Yet amazingly, none of them were bumping into each other. No one seemed to be getting in anyone else's way. There was perfect harmony in the hive.

Yasser and Zahra were impressed.

"Wow! This is awesome. It looks like something out of a science fiction movie!" said Yasser. He looked around at the rows and rows of perfectly shaped and connected hexagons, with the bees moving from one to another, each occupied with a task. "How did you make such an amazing hive?"

Nahla had stopped flying and was now weaving her way through the crowds of bees. "My sisters and I work very hard to build this home. We repair it when it breaks down, we make sure it's warm and that all the eggs can hatch into baby larvae. We look after the larvae till they grow and can join us in our work."

"MashaAllah!" Zahra said. "I think I now understand why we say 'as busy as bees'!"

"And all that is not even half of what we do!" Nahla said.

"What else is there?" asked Zahra.

Nahla walked with them a little deeper into the hive. Further ahead, they saw group of bees who seemed to be standing facing just one area. Because of the activity everywhere else, this small group stood out.

"Do you see those bees?" Nahla asked. "They are serving and protecting our queen. She is the heart of our hive."

The children craned their necks to get a glimpse of the queen and for just a few seconds, when the bees protecting her moved to follow her, they were able to see her.

"She's different to the rest of you," observed Zahra.

"Yes," said Nahla. "She is more elegant and graceful. Allah has made her bigger and longer than us and without her, our hive would not be able to exist."

"What work does she do?" asked Yasser, curious to know. He hadn't seen her look busy at all.

"Work?!" Nahla sounded shocked. "The queen doesn't work! She has to lay eggs so that we can grow as a community and a hive. That is the best and grandest task given to her by Allah. She is our mother. We don't expect her to do anything else for us. My sisters and I serve her, feed her and look after her."

Yasser and Zahra looked at each other. They loved and respected their mother greatly, but they didn't serve her nearly half as well as these bees did!

"HEAVEN IS UNDER THE FEET OF YOUR MOTHER!" Yasser remembered.

"Absolutely!" replied Grandfather, impressed that Yasser had remembered a hadith from the Holy Prophet.

"I guess it's not all about making beautiful cards for Mother's Day," Zahra said. "We need to learn from the bees and treat Mummy well all the time. She deserves it."

Grandfather smiled. He was looking forward to seeing how the children would implement this lesson when they got home.

"How many sisters do you have?" asked Yasser, looking over at Zahra.

"About fifty thousand," Nahla said matter-of-factly. "Although I haven't counted."

"WHAT?" exclaimed Yasser. "Fifty *thousand*?"

"Yes, we have to be many to be able to get all our tasks done and keep the hive alive."

"But don't you guys ever get tired of all the work? Or confused? Or fight with each other?" How do you all fit in this hive without bumping into each other all the time?" Zahra asked.

"We are very organized. From the moment we are born, we know that we have a mission in life and that the only way we can be happy and successful is if each and every one of us does what they have to," Nahla replied.

"That makes so much sense," Yasser said, looking across at Zahra. "I think we need to try some of that when we get back." Zahra smiled and nodded in agreement.

Even difficult tasks become easier when we work together, she thought.

Chapter 19

As they flew around the hive, Zahra kept looking around on either side of Nahla as if she had dropped something and was trying to find it. When the bee felt her moving around, she turned her head and asked, "Is something bothering you, Zahra?"

"It's only that I can't see where all the honey is," Zahra said. "We know bees make honey, but I can't see where you're storing it."

Nahla buzzed in the way they had come to recognize as laughter. "Aaah, our honey! That's what makes us famous, isn't it?"

"We love honey," Yasser said. "It's so sweet and yummy on toast in the morning!"

"And we love making it," Nahla said. "It's one of the most important tasks we have."

"Is it hard to make honey?" Zahra asked, thinking of all the other tasks the bees were already doing.

"Oh, yes, quite hard," replied Nahla. "We first have to fly out to look for flowers that have the sweetest nectar. Once we have found good flowers, we send some bees back home to let the other bees know where to come to get the food. We draw a map to where the flowers are by walking in special patterns that our sisters understand.

"Once we bring the nectar back to the hive, we then mix it with special saliva to make the honey and then we store it in these hexagon cells until it is ready to eat."

"So the honey is in all these little cells?" Zahra asked looking around.

"Yes, the ones that are covered are the ones that are safe to eat from. Each cell is precious because it takes about 400 trips to the flowers and back to collect enough nectar for about half a tablespoon of honey."

"Just half a tablespoon?" Yasser asked. "But we eat so much honey! What's left for you if it's so hard to make and we keep taking it from you?"

"Oh, don't worry," said Nahla. "We make plenty enough for ourselves and lots extra to share as well."

"That's very generous of you," said Zahra. "Thank you, Nahla."

"Alhamdulillah," Nahla said. "This is a task given to us by Allah and we know that our honey is a blessing for human beings and other creatures who eat it, so we do it with love. Now, who would like to taste some of our latest batch of honey?"

"Oh yes, please!" Zahra and Yasser said. They were so excited to taste honey straight from the hive! Nahla opened up the covering from one honeycomb cell and gestured for them to come closer. "Bismillah," she said. They dipped their fingers into the liquid-gold mixture and tasted.

"**MMMMMMMM**." Yasser closed his eyes as the honey melted in his mouth. He hadn't tasted anything like this before!

"This....is.....deeeeelicious!" Zahra said, smacking her lips. "It tastes different to the honey we have at home. It smells like fresh flowers and tastes fruity!"

"I'm glad you like it, Alhamdullilah," Nahla said.

Grandfather had also been busy licking the honey off his fingers. Honey was his most favourite ingredient to put in everything. He loved honey cake, honey-glazed carrots, honey-soaked baklava, honey on toast, honey drizzled over a banana - Grandfather simply couldn't not resist any of it!

He giggled like a child when he saw Yasser and Zahra watching him. Then he said with a cheeky grin, "You know, Prophet Muhammad has said that honey is a remedy for every illness and the Qur'an is a remedy for all illnesses of the mind, so I advise you to use both remedies as often as possible."

"...A DRINK OF DIVERSE HUES COMES FORTH FROM THEIR BELLIES WHEREIN THERE IS A HEALING FOR MANKIND. TRULY THAT IS A SIGN FOR PEOPLE WHO REFLECT," he recited, licking his lips.

Nahla buzzed with excitement. "That's from Surah Nahl as well!"

"Yes!" confirmed Grandfather. "Food scientists have studied honey for years and agree that it has many wonderful benefits."

"But the Qur'an said it first!" Nahla said.

"It did," agreed Grandfather, looking back at Nahla. "You are truly special creatures, which is why Allah mentioned you in His special book!"

Chapter 20

Nahla slowly made her way out of the hive with Grandfather and the children. She told them that she had to drop them off at the exit so they could go to see the next animal. As they flew the distance, Zahra couldn't help commenting, "SubhanAllah! Grandfather is so right, bees are truly amazing!" She gently stroked Nahla's fuzzy hair. "You are such hard workers, so loving and so, so generous!"

"Thank you," Nahla said. "We believe in sharing the blessings of Allah. He is Al-Wadood, the Loving and we love His creatures." She paused for a few seconds and then asked, "Yasser, Zahra, would you be able to give a message to your kind from us?"

"Yes, of course!" the children responded.

"My fellow bees are in trouble around the world," Nahla said. "People are destroying wild flower meadows in order to make room to grow crops. But we need the flowers to survive and make honey! What's worse is that people then spray the crops with pesticides that can kill us or confuse us so that we do not know the way back to our hives.

Thousands of bees are dying every day!" Nahla buzzed, clearly distressed.

"That's horrible!" Zahra said.

"The trouble is, people don't realise that they need us to survive on the planet. We don't just make honey. We also take pollen from one area to another, so we help food and plant life to spread and grow far and wide."

"What kinds of foods?" Yasser asked.

"Apples, apricots, peaches and plums, lemons, limes, cherries, strawberries, raspberries, onions, avocadoes, all types of beans, coffee, oil, grapes, cauliflower, tomatoes, cucumbers..." Nahla paused to take a breath

"That's like...everything!" Yasser said, surprised. He hadn't expected so many fruits and vegetables to be dependent on bees.

"It is unlikely that humans would have enough food to survive on the planet for very long without bees," Grandfather said.

"Please," Nahla said. "Can you get the message to people that they have to **SAVE THE BEES!**"

Yasser and Zahra nodded sincerely. "You have taught us so much, Nahla. Of course, we will do everything we can to make sure you and your kind are safe," Zahra said.

"Thank you," Nahla said, as she lowered herself to the ground gently. "I really hope they listen."

They all said a bitter-sweet goodbye to Nahla. They were glad to have had the chance to see a hive, but saddened with the weight of the knowledge that she had just given them. The zoo was turning out to be an education in so many ways.

Nahla gave them each a drop of honey she had carried with her. "This will help you continue on your journey," she said, looking at Grandfather and giving him a huge wink with her large compound eyes.

No sooner had they sucked on their honey drops than the children began to feel their limbs stretch out and up!

"We're growing!" Zahra cried.

"**HERE WE GOOOOOOOOO!**" Yasser said, laughing out loud.

Once they had got to their normal size, they stretched and looked around, only to see a now tiny Nahla hovering over a flower and then flying off to return to her busy tasks.

Zahra looked down to the blades of grass around her ankles. Just a few moments ago, those same blades of grass had towered over her head. "That was amazing!!" she exclaimed, jumping up and down.

"Grandfather! Look at the Qur'an!!" Yasser cried, pointing and waving.

While they had stopped at their normal size, the Qur'an had continued to grow bigger and bigger until it now towered over Grandfather and the children like a gateway into a new and exciting world. The Holy Book opened, its giant words of wisdom giving out a soft, warm glow. Zahra was mesmerised by the text. *Now I know why you get rewards for just looking at the Qur'an*, she thought.

The pages turned to the twenty-ninth surah. "That's Surah Ankaboot!" Yasser said, then his expression changed as he slowly translated, "The... spider..."

Zahra couldn't contain her elation. "Our next exhibit is spiders! Alhamdullilah! I was so hoping we would go there!"

They waited for the giant Qur'an to shut, and as it did, it returned to its usual size. Grandfather lovingly kissed it and returned it to his pocket. He then pulled out the zoo map to figure out the way to the spiders.

"We're moving north," announced Grandfather. As they began their walk down the path, Zahra skipped ahead, but Yasser was strangely quiet. He walked close to Grandfather and held his hand tight. He was not looking forward to the next stop!

ankaboot

Chapter 21

The walk from the bees to the Spider Exhibition was down another tree-lined avenue and Yasser could feel fear creeping into his veins. *Why do spiders have to be so scary?* he thought. He decided to distract himself by asking a question that had been on his mind since they had first seen the camels.

"Jamal and Naaqa told us about all the special features camels have so that they can live in the desert and it's amazing how complex life in Nahla's hive is. I wonder, does Allah have a reason for *everything* that He made?"

"Good question," Grandfather remarked. He had noticed Yasser's odd reluctance to go to their next stop. Although he had an idea what the reason could be, Grandfather hoped that learning about Allah's Majesty might ease whatever was bothering Yasser.

He cleared his throat. "Allah is al-Musawwir, the Fashioner. He shapes and designs everything in a particular way. In fact, He asks us many times in the Qur'an to look at how perfectly He has created the world around us." Grandfather paused, feeling a tingle down his spine at the thought of Allah's design. He reached for his Qur'an and began browsing its pages. Zahra who had noticed they had stopped, jogged back.

"What's happening?" she asked. "We need to hurry."

"Grandfather is looking for a verse for me," Yasser explained.

Zahra bounced gently on her toes. She wanted to go and see the spiders, but she was also curious to know what Grandfather would find.

"Ah, here it is," Grandfather pointed to the verses in the Qur'an. He lovingly touched the blessed words and glided his finger along the lines as he recited, first in Arabic and then the translation:

"VERILY, IN THE CREATION OF THE HEAVENS AND THE EARTH AND THE ALTERNATION OF THE NIGHT AND THE DAY ARE SIGNS FOR THOSE OF UNDERSTANDING;

WHO REMEMBER ALLAH WHILE
STANDING OR SITTING OR LYING
ON THEIR SIDES AND GIVE
THOUGHT TO THE CREATION OF
THE HEAVENS AND THE EARTH,
SAYING: OUR LORD, YOU DID
NOT CREATE THIS AIMLESSLY;
EXALTED ARE YOU ABOVE SUCH A
THING, THEN PROTECT US FROM
THE PUNISHMENT OF THE FIRE."

"These are from Surah Ale Imran."

"So, nothing pointless or by chance," Yasser confirmed.

"Not a single thing," Grandfather said firmly, shutting the Qur'an and taking each child's hand. They began walking again and everyone was quiet for a while.

Zahra was deep in thought and then she laughed as she realised something. "If someone remembers Allah when they are sitting, standing and lying on their sides, that means that they are always remembering Allah!"

"Exactly!" Grandfather said. "It means whatever situation we are in, we should remember Allah!

Sometimes it's through our prayers, sometimes through our du'a and sometimes we just think about Him in our hearts."

Zahra was silent for a moment. "I think I forgot about Allah this morning when I was complaining about being bored," she said, looking ashamed.

"I forget a lot of times too," Yasser told her, patting her arm.

"We all do," Grandfather said. "The important thing is to try and keep reminders around us and to be conscious all the time so that we come back to remembering. That's why we have our daily prayers and recommended tasbihaat. To remind us to think about Him."

"Look!" cried Zahra, waving her arms and pointing ahead. "A giant web!"

Sure enough, they were coming up to the archway entrance of the next exhibition and above it was the biggest web they had ever seen. It stretched from end to end and woven in the centre of it were the words

'QASR AL-ANKABOOT'

Chapter 21

"Castle of the Spiders," translated Zahra in a hushed whisper, her eyes wide and sparkling. They were all standing at the entrance and she was straining her neck to see the entire web masterpiece. "I wonder how many spiders worked together to make that web... or maybe it was one huge spider!"

Yasser let out a whimper. He pressed his face into Grandfather's tummy and tried really hard not to throw up. He was terrified of spiders. He had never told anyone, but whenever he saw one scuttle along the floor or hang suspended in mid-air, a chill would run down his spine.

Grandfather gently peeled him away and knelt down so that he could look him in the eye. "What's wrong Yasser? Are you okay?"

Yasser shook his head. "I... I... I don't like spiders."

"But they are amazing!" Zahra said. "They are so clever and look at the beautiful webs they make!"

Grandfather looked at Zahra and then back at Yasser sympathetically. "Yasser, most spiders are harmless and all the spiders at this exhibition are safe."

"I know that," said Yasser. "And I also know I'm waaaay bigger than them. Except maybe the spider that made that web, and I'm not afraid of snakes or bees, it just spiders." He let out a wail. "But I can't help it. I really, really don't like them."

"That's okay too," Grandfather said. " A lot of people feel uneasy around spiders."

"I don't," said Zahra.

Both Grandfather and Yasser looked over at Zahra.

"I didn't mean to make you feel bad Yasser!" she said apologetically. "I only meant that I can help you. I'll walk ahead and if any spiders come near us, I'll speak to them so they don't come near you."

"Thank you, Zahra." Yasser smiled at the thought of his baby sister protecting him. He went to her and gave a quick hug. "I'm sure you'll be a big help."

"I'll try my best," Zahra promised sincerely. She had felt how fast Yasser's heart was beating and knew he really was scared.

"Let's all take a few deep breaths to calm ourselves before we go meet these wondrous creatures," Grandfather suggested. He counted to three and they all took deep breaths through their noses and let them out through their mouths.

"I do feel a bit better," Yasser said. "But we haven't actually seen a spider yet...."

"Let me tell you one more secret to being calm and peaceful," Grandfather said, smiling. "Allah tells us in Surah Ra'ad that **'TRULY IN THE REMEMBRANCE OF ALLAH DO THE HEARTS FIND PEACE'**."

"Just like we were talking about," Zahra added, clapping her hands.

"Go on," said Grandfather, gently. "Try it."

Yasser took another deep breath. "Allah created me and He created spiders... and He will look after me." Yasser said in a loud whisper and immediately felt a soothing calm settle in his belly. He looked up at Grandfather and took his hand tightly. "I can do this." The look in his eye was determined and he even managed a small smile. "Bismilllah, let's go in."

Zahra led the way, looking behind every so often. She could see Yasser's lips moving as he repeated dhikr and although his face was white and withdrawn, when he caught her eye, he gave her a smile and a nod. She felt a huge surge of pride for her brother's bravery and sent up a prayer in her heart, '*O Allah, let me be able to help him in whatever way he needs.*'

Chapter 22

As they walked along the expansive exhibition, they saw many different varieties of spider, each living in a different habitat. The zoo was truly extraordinary, showcasing all the different environments in the world, but right next to each other.

They passed one spider busily weaving a web under the shadowy eaves of a house. A little way ahead was another spider webbing in the garden. On the opposite side of the path, they saw a spider gliding along the surface of a pond and another diving below the water looking for food.

"Whoa! Did you see that, Grandfather?" Yasser asked, astonished. "Did you see that spider dive into the water like a torpedo? That was so cool, mashaAllah!"

Grandfather nodded. "Yes, some spiders spin webs to catch their food, but others have to go hunting for their prey."

"Are the divers looking for fish?" Zahra asked.

She had never heard of spiders eating fish, but you could never tell what secrets were hidden in this zoo.

"No, my dear, not fish." Grandfather laughed. "All spiders eat insects. Did you know that spiders keep the insect population under control by eating them? If they didn't, the whole world would be covered in insects!"

"Seriously?" asked Zahra. She made a face at the thought of being swarmed by insects of all kinds.

"Yes! A spider eats about two thousand insects every year. If they didn't, those insects would eat our crops and ruin harvests. **WE WOULDN'T BE ABLE TO SURVIVE WITHOUT SPIDERS**. And they also serve as food for other small animals like lizards, toads and birds"

"Grandfather, how do you know all this?" Yasser asked. He was now feeling intrigued by spiders and also guilty for being scared of them instead of grateful to them.

"**IQRA - READ!** It was the first verse of the Holy Qur'an that was revealed. Reading is the key to opening up a world of opportunities and lessons."

Zahra pulled out her notebook. She drew a spider and then some small bugs and a lizard. Then she drew more lines from one to the other. "SubhanAllah!" she said, when she finished. **"EVERYTHING IS CONNECTED!** Every creature big or small has a job, a purpose and a role to play"

Yasser leaned over to see his sister's notebook. "This looks like a pattern," he observed, tracing the connecting lines with his finger.

"It is," agreed Grandfather, looking over her shoulder at her drawing. "It's Allah's Perfectly Planned Pattern. In fact, what you have made is actually a food web."

"Well, it can't be better than the webs I make," a thin voice said from above, making them all jump in surprise.

Chapter 23

"Asalaamu alaykum!" the voice called out.

Zahra looked up, peering through the foliage until she could see the little brown spider hanging upside down from a fine silver thread. Yasser moved behind Grandfather and peeked out from his side, reciting his dhikr a little faster under his breath.

"Wa alaykum asalaam," called out Grandfather. "Are you our guide?"

"Yes, that's me. Your guide." The spider slid down smoothly, extending its line of silk until it was hanging level with Zahra's face. "My name is Ankaboot. What's yours?"

"I'm Zahra. This is my Grandfather and that's my brother, Yasser."

"Welcome, welcome!" The spider had a high-pitched voice and talked a little fast, repeating words as if it needed to emphasize what it was saying. "Why why is your brother hiding? Doesn't he want to see our world? " The spider swung forward as if she wanted to get a closer look at Yasser.

Zahra quickly stepped in its way. "He's just a little shy. But don't worry, he'll see and listen and learn, just like I will. We want to know more about the insects Allah has created."

"Well, for starters then, did you know that a spider is *not* actually an insect? We are part of the arachnid family, which means we have eight legs and two body parts instead of six legs and three body parts like insects do. Eight and two. Not six and three. We also don't have backbones, wings or antennae." Ankaboot indicated to her back as if to prove her point, "Look! No wings."

Zahra wondered if Ankaboot had repeated the part about not having wings because she wished she had some, but her doubts were soon laid to rest.

"Who needs wings when we can make webs! **WHEEEE**!" Ankaboot shot out a silver thread to the nearby tree, and swung over, moving ahead and forcing them to follow her deeper into the exhibition.

She carried on chattering as she walked and swung. "Eight legs and eight eyes as well. Most of us have eight eyes, but some of us have less. You would think we could see everything with eight eyes, right? But not really. We can only see things that are nearby. But that's okay too, because we can hear vibrations through the hair on our legs so we can keep up with what's happening around us!"

Zahra was fascinated and Yasser seemed curious too. "That's really amazing, Ankaboot," he said.

Ankaboot paused, happy to see Yasser looking a bit more relaxed. She was keen to show him more about the wonders of spiders! "Let me tell you more about my kind," she carried on. "Our skeletons are on the outside of our bodies instead of skin. As we grow, we moult. That means every time we increase in size, we have to shed our old skeleton skin so the new one can take its place. We moult many times before becoming adults and some of us moult regularly all our lives."

"Your skeleton skin is called an exoskeleton, right?" Yasser asked, remembering that from his science lessons.

"That's absolutely correct!" Ankaboot said.

Yasser blushed, but he felt good too. Talking spiders weren't as scary as spiders that just crawled around without telling you what they were planning to do.

Chapter 24

Ankaboot stopped at a tree that had a lot of branches. She perched on a branch and held up her front legs. "We have now reached the main event at the Spider Exhibition!" she announced grandly. "Yes, reached!"

"I think I can guess what it is," Zahra said, clapping her hands. "You're going to make a web!"

"Not just any web! A grand web! A majestic web!"

"But you're so tiny," Yasser couldn't help saying.

"Great things come in small packages, boy, great things!" Ankaboot retorted. "I am a garden spider and I make orb webs. Round ones, shiny and filled with light!"

Zahra looked at Yasser and smiled. It seemed that Ankaboot enjoyed adding some drama to her tour. They watched in wonder as Ankaboot began to pull silk out of her spinnerets. She was concentrating very hard and began by building a single line like a bridge from one branch to another. Then she added more lines until she had a four-sided frame. Finally, she began to make diagonal spokes from one end to the other that intersected in the middle.

"SubhanAllah!" Yasser gasped.

"How has she hidden all that thread in her belly?" Zahra wondered.

"She hasn't," said Grandfather, leaning down to whisper to them so that he wouldn't distract Ankaboot from her work. "The silk is stored as liquid in her belly and her body constantly produces it. When she pulls it out and the breeze hits it, it instantly becomes solid."

"Oh." Zahra stared back at Ankaboot, who was busy adding the circular threads that would form the main body of the web. She had never seen something this wonderful in action and her mind felt like exploding with amazement at how everything was perfectly in place.

"But Grandfather, don't spiders catch bugs in their webs?" Yasser asked. When Grandfather nodded, he continued. "Then how is it that they don't get stuck on the threads as they build them?" He pointed to Ankaboot who was scuttling along the web lines gracefully and without a single stumble.

"Well, the threads Ankaboot is spinning are of two kinds, sticky and non-sticky. She knows which ones to step on and which ones to avoid. That's all part of..."

"**ALLAH'S PERFECT DESIGN!**" both children finished.

"All done!" Ankaboot declared, calling their attention back the web. "Ta-da!"

For a few seconds, the children were confused. Standing under the shadowy trees, they couldn't really see much. Then a gentle breeze blew and allowed the sunlight to filter down through the leaves. Suddenly, right in front of them a gorgeous, sparkling network of silk threads appeared. It twinkled and glistened in the sunlight.

"It truly is a majestic work!" Grandfather said.

"It's magical!" Zahra added.

Yasser could only nod. He had never felt like this before. Both uneasy of the creature who was the artist as well as in awe of the artwork it had produced.

"I'm glad you like it, so glad," Ankaboot said. She sounded pleased as she sat on the web, swaying slightly with it. "It's not just a pretty piece of work though. Not just pretty. My web is made of silk threads that are stronger than steel! Stronger! And once a bug gets stuck in it, there's no getting out. None at all!"

Ankaboot quickly crawled to the edge of the web and disappeared into the leaves. Her muffled voice carried down to them, "Coming down. Down I'm coming."

As they wait for her to appear again, Yasser tugged at Grandfather's sleeve. "If spider silk is so strong, why do their webs break so easily?"

Grandfather quickly put a finger to his lips and hushed him. "I'll explain later," he whispered.

Ankaboot suddenly swung in front of their faces again. Yasser let out a little cry and stepped back. "Don't do that!"

Zahra quickly came to stand between the spider and her brother. "I told you not to go near him. Please be careful."

"Sorry, sorry," Ankaboot climbed back up a little way. "I don't bite!"

"Sorry." Yasser sighed, realising he had overreacted. "You just surprised me," he said.

"I have a surprise as well! A surprise story! Do you want to hear it?"

"Yes please! We love stories," the children exclaimed.

"Long, long ago, when the Prophet Muhammad was alive, he had to migrate from Makkah to Medina because the enemies of Islam wanted to harm him."

"The hijrah!" Zahra said.

"Yes, yes! He left Makkah at night and had to stop along the way and take shelter in a cave. While he was inside, the enemies came along looking for him so Allah commanded one of our own to build a web across the opening of the cave. When the enemies reached the cave, they saw the web and thought there was no way the Prophet could be inside, because otherwise the web would have been broken. So, they left the cave and carried on searching for him elsewhere!"

"A spider saved the Prophet with his web!" Yasser loved this story.

"Well, actually, Allah saved the Prophet through the spider-web. Everything in this world serves Allah," Grandfather replied.

"Everything serves Allah," Ankaboot agreed.

How do I serve Allah? Zahra wondered. She realised that it was a very important question and the answer to it would hold the key to her future.

Chapter 25

Suddenly, there was a rustle and a rumble and a thrashing of wings as a flock of birds flew low across the path.

"Look out!" yelled Yasser, but it was too late. One of the birds flew right into the web that Ankaboot had just finished weaving and tore a chunk of it off with its beak!

"Ya Allah!" Zahra cried. "Oh no, Ankaboot!" Tears welled up in her eyes as she saw the shreds of silk hanging from the gaping hole in the web.

Yasser looked similarly disturbed, but when they looked at Ankaboot, they were surprised to see her staring back at them calmly.

"Why do you cry?" she asked. "Why tears, Zahra?"

"All your hard work! It's been destroyed."

"No it's not. It's just a hole. A little hole," said Ankaboot. "I can fix it just now. My webs break all the time. Why sometimes, I make a web, then take it down at night and build it again the next morning! Worry not, children, these things are temporary! No worry!"

Yasser and Zahra looked from Ankaboot to Grandfather, not quite sure how to respond to this.

"Isn't your web your home?" asked Grandfather gently. "How do you feel safe if it can be destroyed so easily?"

"Safe?" Ankaboot made a sound that sounded like a laugh. "We are kept safe by Allah! We have no fear when we know He is with us."

Grandfather smiled a big smile. That was exactly what he had hoped the spider would say. "MashaAllah, Ankaboot. May Allah keep your faith strong and pray for us to be the same."

"Of course," said Ankaboot, although she sounded surprised that anyone would doubt the protection of Allah at any time. "Now I must fix this web and you must go along on your journey. I can't accompany you to the exit, but if you follow this path, you will find your way out in a few minutes."

"Thank you, Ankaboot!" said Zahra. "For sharing your life and showing us your wonderful skills."

"Shukran," said Yasser. "You really are an amazing creature."

"Oh, that's very polite and kind," Ankaboot said, letting out another spidery laugh. "Now off you go or you'll run out of time!" And with that she scurried away to climb the tree and get back to the tattered web.

Chapter 26

As soon as they were out of earshot, Yasser turned to Grandfather. "You said you would explain about why webs break so easily even though the silk they are made of is so strong."

"And why don't they feel bad about their hard work being destroyed?" added Zahra.

Grandfather took out his Qur'an again and this time he opened it as they continued walking. "Let me read out to you from Surah Ankaboot," he said.

"THE PARABLE OF THOSE WHO TAKE PROTECTORS APART FROM ALLAH IS THAT OF THE SPIDER THAT MAKES A HOUSE. TRULY THE FRAILEST OF HOUSES IS THE SPIDER'S HOUSE, IF THEY BUT KNEW. TRULY ALLAH KNOWS WHATSOEVER THEY CALL UPON APART FROM HIM. HE IS THE MIGHTY, THE WISE."

"What's a parapebble?" asked Zahra.

"Para -bal," corrected Grandfather. "It means a simple story that teaches a lesson through examples."

"So…the Qur'an is comparing people who don't have faith in Allah, who rely on other things rather than Allah, to a spider and its web. I think Allah wants us to understand that a spider's web is delicate and not as strong as the spiders think it is," Zahra declared

"Maybe Allah is trying to tell us that when we build our hopes around people or other things instead of Him, our hopes and wishes can easily break, because He is the only protector and helper for the believers," said Yasser.

"Yes," said Grandfather, nodding. "And not just people, but things as well. Sometimes, we feel that if we have money, we will be safe. Or that our education and intellect will keep us safe. But everything can be lost or become useless in a second. Only those who seek protection sincerely from Allah will find peace even in the most difficult situations."

"Like Imam Husayn did on the Day of Ashura…." Yasser remembered. "Even though he was facing a vicious army ready to attack him, he was calm and patient through everything."

"And Lady Zainab," added Zahra, recalling the serenity they had seen on her beautiful face.

"It's wonderful that you remembered the Imam at such a time," Grandfather said, giving each of them a tight squeeze.

They walked along quietly for a while, each lost in their own thoughts, until they reached another archway like the one they had entered from and emerged on the other side onto a sunny pathway.

"We're back in the main zoo, I think," said Yasser, stretching out and basking in the warmth of the sun. He hadn't realised how tense he had been through the entire walk through the spiders' territory.

"You seem less uneasy about spiders," Grandfather observed.

"I am," Yasser said. "I mean, I am glad to be out of there," he pointed backwards, "but I decided to learn from Ankaboot and place my full trust in Allah. He will protect me from my fears."

"You're the bestest, bravest big brother in the world!" Zahra said, hugging Yasser, who laughed and then pulled away, a little red in the face.

"The more I learn about Allah's magnificent

creations, the more I want to learn about them," he said. "I still don't like spiders, but I can definitely see how useful they are and how they serve a purpose in the world."

"I think they are master artists," said Zahra. "I wish I could make webs like them!"

They all laughed as Zahra twirled around, weaving her arms and pretending to hang invisible silk threads in the air.

Just then a familiar hum rose from Grandfather's pocket.

"The Qur'an!" they exclaimed. "Our next stop!"

They looked on eagerly as Grandfather took out the already-glowing Qur'an and waited for it to open and show them their next stop. When the book did open, one chapter lifted off the page and began to shine with a greater intensity. Grandfather, Yasser and Zahra gasped.

"Look!" Zahra said in awe. "There are five verses in this surah!"

"It's Surah Feel," Yasser said.

"To the Elephant Exhibition!" Grandfather declared.

feel

ELEPHANT
EXHIBITION

Chapter 27

"FFFEHUUUURRRRRH!"

"Did you hear that Yasser?" Zahra nudged her brother. "I think we're almost there!"

Yasser could hear a faint rumbling in the distance and the trumpeting was getting a lot louder. They turned one more corner and a huge archway came into view.

"This is it. Our final stop!" Grandfather confirmed.

They rushed over to a huge sign at the entrance that was filled with interesting information about the animal they had come to see.

"Wow!" Yasser said, reading from the sign. "Did you know that the African elephant is the world's largest land mammal?"

THE ELEPHANT

Elephant's are ALWAYS hungry. They eat can 150kgs of food in a day!

The world's LARGEST land mammal

Elephants have 150,000 muscles in their trunk!

Elephants have their own sunscreen! After a swamp bath, they'll throw mud and sand up onto themselves to protect their skin from the hot hot sun

As he spoke, the leaves in the trees around them began to rustle. "Shhh, did you hear that?" Yasser asked, his voice barely a whisper.

"Was it the wind?" Zahra asked, listening closer.

"I don't think so." Yasser was sure it sounded more deliberate. "There it is again! It's coming from over there!" he said, pointing to a clump of trees on their right.

As they cautiously approached the rustling trees, a telescopic elephant trunk pierced through the leaves and trumpeted loudly at them! Yasser and Zahra closed their eyes and quickly clapped their hands over their ears. When they finally recovered and opened their eyes, a **HUGE** elephant stood in front of them.

"Asalaamu alykum!" he said with a cheeky grin. "My name is Feel and I'm your exhibition guide!"

Yasser and Zahra stood on either side of Grandfather, who was watching and listening with a huge smile on his face. The children strained their necks back and looked up.

"You're humongous! Colossal! Enormous! Gargantuan!" cried Yasser.

"Haha! Thank you, I *feel* pretty great too" He let out another trumpet. "Get it? Feel?" His whole body shook as he laughed at his own joke. Zahra giggled. Another cheerful animal! Yasser was getting plenty of company for his jokes.

"I can't wait tell you more about myself," said Feel. "But do you have any questions before we begin?"

The children hesitated.

"Don't be afraid. We might be big, but we aren't dangerous. You can ask me anything, anything at all!" Feel said. "After all, the Holy Prophet told us **KNOWLEDGE HAS A LOCK ON IT AND ITS KEY IS ASKING QUESTIONS**."

Yasser smiled and his eyes twinkled mischievously. "Is it true," he asked, "that you can eat a hundred and fifty kilograms of food in a day?" Yasser had read the fact on the sign and still couldn't believe it. "You must have an active digestive system!"

Zahra laughed hard. "That's his way of asking if you do a lot of poo!" she said between her giggles.

Yasser blushed, a little embarrassed, but he was still curious. "So...do you?"

"Well, we spend sixteen hours a day eating, so yes, of course we need to digest all that food and use it up. In fact, we can eat double that amount if we're really hungry," said Feel. "So I can make about one tonne of poo a week!"

"ONE TONNE?" Yasser felt faint.

"EVERY WEEK?" added Zahra, feeling a little sick at the thought.

"Isn't it amazing?" said Feel, puffing out his chest and flexing his trunk.

"You seem awfully proud of it," said Zahra.

Yasser nudged Zahra. "Wouldn't you be proud of a one tonne poo, Zahra?" he said, trying hard not to laugh.

"Of course I'm proud of it!" said Feel. "Our poo - or dung as we like to call it - is very, very important. It keeps the soil fertile and disperses tree seeds. We eat lots of different plants and fruits and then walk for miles each day. Our fertile dung piles are full of seeds that allow plants to grow in new areas. Over ninety species of trees rely on us for propagation!"

Zahra thought of all the leafy avenues they had walked down and Nahla's flowery paradise. How could such beautiful things come to being through the help of something so yucky? Her understanding of the world and how it worked was changing ever so slowly. "SubhanAllah!" she remarked. "Allah has thought of everything!"

Chapter 28

As Feel turned around to lead them further into the exhibition, the children couldn't help but notice how gracefully he moved for such a large creature. Yasser and Zahra followed with Grandfather.

After a few minutes, Zahra spoke up. "You know how we always used to sing that rhyme about stomping elephants?" she asked Yasser. "We can't even hear Feel's footsteps. I thought the trees would be shaking with the sound of his marching."

"You watch too many cartoons," Yasser retorted.

Zahra smiled widely. She did like cartoons!

"Why don't you ask Feel?" Grandfather gently pushed Zahra forward. "He doesn't mind answering your questions."

Zahra walked ahead so she was near the elephant's head. "Excuse me... Feel?" Zahra said shyly.

"Yes, my dear?" Feel looked directly at her and she could see his beautiful, soulful eyes lined with soft, long lashes.

"Could you please tell us how you walk so softly?" Zahra asked.

"Oh, it's because we walk on our toes. The soles of our feet are made of fatty tissue and our toes are buried inside this tissue. This allows us to walk quietly."

"I don't think I could walk on my toes all day," Zahra said. She tried walking on her tippy-toes in circles around Grandfather, but couldn't do more than a few turns.

"Zahra, look at this!" Yasser called out. He was standing behind them all with both feet inside one of Feel's footprints.

"Oh wow!" Zahra exclaimed, coming over. "Feel, your footprints are huge!"

"Yes, they are!" Feel nodded. "When they fill with rain water, they become little ponds in which beetles, worms, tadpoles and other small creatures live."

"That's amazing!" Zahra exclaimed. She was astounded at how such a huge animal like Feel could play a part in the survival of tiny creatures like worms and beetles, as well as the plants and fruits that surrounded them. "Everything is connected," she whispered to herself.

Chapter 29

"Welcome to my home!" Feel announced.

Yasser and Zahra looked around at the swampy marshland that stretched out ahead of them. In the distance, black silhouettes of trees framed the horizon. The soft rumble of other elephants surrounded them. Their eyes were immediately drawn to a group of elephants that was approaching them.

"That's my herd," said Feel. "My family."

"They look so much bigger than they do on television or in books," Yasser said.

"They're majestic," whispered Zahra, mesmerised by their swaying trunks and swinging tails. The herd lumbered slowly towards them, as if they didn't have a care in the world.

Feel led the children and Grandfather to meet the herd halfway and they gathered together under the shade of some fig trees. Zahra and Yasser watched in amazement as Feel rested on his hind legs, placed his fore legs on a tree and then used his trunk to reach high up into its branches. He delicately pulled aside the leaves and picked off fruits, offering them to Grandfather, Yasser and Zahra first and then fetching some more for himself. His family helped themselves as well.

They rested and ate the delicious figs. Feel's family then joined him in making a circle around Grandfather and the children. After a low rumble, the elephants began to recite in a melodious chorus:

بِسْمِ ٱللَّهِ ٱلرَّحْمَٰنِ ٱلرَّحِيمِ

أَلَمْ تَرَ كَيْفَ فَعَلَ رَبُّكَ بِأَصْحَٰبِ ٱلْفِيلِ ﴿١﴾

أَلَمْ يَجْعَلْ كَيْدَهُمْ فِى تَضْلِيلٍ ﴿٢﴾

وَأَرْسَلَ عَلَيْهِمْ طَيْرًا أَبَابِيلَ ﴿٣﴾

تَرْمِيهِم بِحِجَارَةٍ مِّن سِجِّيلٍ ﴿٤﴾

فَجَعَلَهُمْ كَعَصْفٍ مَّأْكُولٍ ﴿٥﴾

IN THE NAME OF ALLAH, THE KIND THE MERCIFUL

HAVE YOU NOT REGARDED HOW YOUR LORD DEALT WITH THE PEOPLE OF THE ELEPHANT?

DID HE NOT MAKE THEIR PLOTS GO WRONG,

AND SENT AGAINST THEM FLOCKS OF BIRDS,

PELTING THEM WITH STONES OF SHALE,

THUS MAKING THEM LIKE CHEWED UP STRAW?

When they finished the recitation, there was a moment of absolute silence and then Zahra and Yasser both let out an audible sigh.

"That was absolutely beautiful!" Zahra said.

"Surah Feel recited by elephants...incredible!" Yasser added.

Feel smiled at their looks of wonder. "Yes, we are very honoured that Allah named an entire chapter of the Qur'an after us. Let me tell you the story behind the surah!"

Yasser and Zahra shuffled to sit more comfortably. There was nothing they enjoyed more than stories from the Qur'an. Today had been so special for them, hearing about the people of Thamud from Naaqa, seeing Firawn and the magicians with Thu'baan, and now they were learning about the people of the Elephant from Feel!

Feel took centre stage ready to begin. "Surah Feel is all about Abraha, an Abyssinian king from Yemen. He was jealous of the number of pilgrims who went to visit the Kaaba every year and so he built a magnificent church in San'a to try and stop people from going to Makkah."

"Did it work?" Zahra asked.

"No, it didn't. In fact, some of the Arabs even dishonoured his church," replied Feel.

"That must have made Abraha very cross," Zahra commented.

"Yes, it made him really angry. He made that a

pretext to destroy the Kaaba. He brought together the largest army in Arabia and some of our elephant ancestors. He wanted the elephants to break down the walls of the Holy House of Allah!" Feel said.

"Well, I can see why Abraha wanted to have elephants in his army. When I first saw you Feel, I was a little scared too. Imagine how the people in Makkah must have felt when they saw an army of elephants!" exclaimed Zahra.

"They were terrified! They had never seen such animals and in such large numbers. It was a truly a sight to behold."

"But what did the elephants do?" asked Yasser, dying to know.

"When the leader of the elephants, who was called Mahmud, reached the boundaries of the haram, he refused to step inside. Instead, he knelt down out of respect."

"Oh!" Zahra felt warm inside. How proud you must be of Mahmud!

Feel continued, "Allah then sent swarms of birds from every direction with stones in their claws! They dropped the stones on the army and destroyed them."

"SubhanAllah! Allah protected the Kaaba and ruined Abraha's plan!" Zahra said.

"Massive creatures like elephants and small creatures like birds all working together under Allah's command. Wonderful!" Yasser added.

"It's a lesson for us all," said Grandfather. "Allah is the Best of Planners. If He chooses to protect something or someone, then no one can harm it! And if He decides to destroy something or someone, no one can stop Him!"

"It doesn't matter how powerful you think you are in the world, Allah is the Most Powerful," Zahra said.

"This event became a famous story in Arabia. That year was named **AAMUL FEEL, THE YEAR OF THE ELEPHANT!** And guess what? Later that year Prophet Muhammad was born," said Feel.

Zahra clapped her hands. "That's perfect! Allah kept His house and his prophet safe in the same year."

"Sadly, even though the story was so famous, most of the Arabs did not learn any lessons from it. They still didn't revere Allah, the Lord of the Kaaba. They continued to fill the holy place with their own idols," Grandfather said. "It was many years later after the Prophet returned with Islam to Makkah that the Kaaba was finally free of idols."

Yasser began to scribble furiously in his notebook. He did not want to forget the lessons he had learnt today. Zahra did the same, making her own observations and notes.

Chapter 30

When Zahra had closed her notebook, she looked closely at Feel and the other elephants again. Her heart was filled with love for these complex animals. She put her book away and walked over to Feel who was standing in the shade; his trunk swaying, lost in thought.

Zahra stood next to one of his thick legs and stared at the saggy, creased skin, the grooves and wrinkles forming intricate patterns. Suddenly, she pressed her face against his leg and hugged him tightly. His rough skin brushed against her soft cheek, but she didn't mind. "Thank you Allah, for creating these wonderful animals!" she said softly.

"JazakAllah for the hug, Zahra," Feel said. "I wish all people would love us like you do."

"What do you mean?" she asked, wondering how anyone could fail to love these gentle giants.

Feel's eyes saddened. "Come, let me show you," he said, leading them all to a box hidden away under a tree. Feel used his trunk to open the box and picked out three funny-looking glasses. He handed one to each of them. "These are special visors. When you put them on, you will have a glimpse of the future of this planet and the creatures that live here."

"A chance to look into the future?" Yasser quickly put on the futuristic goggles. Grandfather and Zahra followed suit. The visors were like 3D goggles with a strap that fastened behind their heads.

The scene around them changed dramatically and Yasser had to hold out his arms to balance against the unsteady feeling. It was alarming to see the world transform so dramatically before their eyes. Luscious green leaves and sparkling streams had been replaced by abandoned grey smoky buildings and cracked arid earth. The temperature felt hotter, the air was stifling and breathing was uncomfortable.

"Where are you, Feel?" Zahra asked, looking towards him, but seeing only empty space and more debris.

"This is the future," Feel replied. "You cannot see me there because elephants are extinct."

"**EXTINCT?**" Yasser gasped. "Why? How?" he asked bewildered.

"Right now, poachers kill around a hundred elephants each day for the ivory our tusks are made of. They also sell our skins to make leather ."

I've always loved the look of ivory jewellery, Zahra thought, feeling guilty that she had never once thought of where the ivory had come from.

"I used to have cousins in the Middle East, in Indonesia, northern Africa and China, but not anymore." Feel took a deep breath. "What you see is the future if this behaviour continues."

Yasser clenched his fists in anger. "How do poachers do this?" he asked. "And why do we let them get away with it?"

"Where are all the other animals?" Zahra asked, not sure she wanted to hear the answer.

"You see, it's not only poachers that have caused the problem," Feel said, sadly looking around the savannah. "As the number of people on the earth increases, so does your need for space. Humans have been destroying our natural habitats to make their cities larger and to grow crops, but animals cannot survive without safe places to live, and food to eat."

Zahra remembered Nahla's warning and the food web she had drawn with Ankaboot, "Everything is connected," she remembered. Without animals, how would humans survive?

Yasser was thinking about what Feel had said earlier, about how his footprints were a home for smaller animals and that without his dung, plant life would not be able to spread. He crinkled his forehead, confused, "Is that why there are hardly any plants here?"

Zahra looked around and realised the fig trees they had just sat under had been cut down to make way for these buildings.

"Yes," replied Feel. "It works both ways. Animals need plants for shelter and food, and plants need animals to propagate and grow. Deforestation has meant that many of the earth's forests and jungles have been destroyed."

Yasser had learnt about deforestation at school. "Isn't deforestation one of the main reasons for global warming?" he asked.

"That's absolutely right." Feel said.

"Why is the earth all dry and cracked?" Zahra asked, concerned.

"Without trees, the soil has no protection from the sun so it becomes cracked and dry," Feel replied. "Come this way," he said ominously, "there's still more to see."

Before they could take another step forward, they heard a familiar hum emanating from Grandfather's pocket.

"The Qur'an!" exclaimed Zahra, "I think it is guiding us to something."

Grandfather swiftly pulled out the Qur'an. Glowing in his hands, the covers swung open forcefully. Smoky clouds gathered above them as a verse lifted itself off the page.

"CORRUPTION HAS SPREAD ON LAND AND SEA AS A RESULT OF WHAT PEOPLE'S HANDS HAVE DONE, SO THAT ALLAH MAY CAUSE THEM TO TASTE THE CONSEQUENCES OF SOME OF THEIR DEEDS AND PERHAPS THEY MIGHT RETURN TO THE RIGHT PATH."

Yasser and Zahra gasped in awe. Grandfather shook his head knowingly. "The Holy Qur'an brings good news and is a warner for mankind."

Yasser gently placed his palm over the pages. They had continued to be surprised by the wisdom in the Qur'an. "This is not ordinary book." he whispered in realisation. "It is a...miracle."

"What do you mean?" Zahra asked.

"Well, look at the words," Yasser said, pointing to the pages. "They are the same in the future as they were in the past, so it never changes. It can predict the future and it is so..." Yasser waved his hands looking for the words to express his sentiment, "so... powerful." He paused. "Like it talks right to you."

Zahra nodded in agreement. The Qur'an really is a miracle, she thought. She remembered how accurately the Qur'an had recounted stories from the past prophets, and how it was the Qur'an that has first told people about honey being a cure for sicknesses.

Grandfather smiled. He was pleased that Yasser and Zahra were finally realising the truly miraculous nature of the Qur'an. Just then, they heard Feel call.

Yasser, Zahra and Grandfather followed Feel's voice to where the stream had once been. There, they saw a small trickle of murky water, much smaller than the clear, glistening stream they had seen earlier.

Yasser gasped. "Look at all the rubbish! It looks like a dustbin has exploded!" he said, pointing to the plastic packets and bags where there had once been pure, clean water.

Some netting, similar to what oranges are packaged in, was moving strangely in the water. It caught Zahra's eye and as she walked closer, a terrible sight confronted her. Inside the netting, there was a snake wriggling and trying to escape, but it was trapped and completely helpless.

"Grandfather!" she cried, "This snake needs our help!"

Grandfather and Yasser rushed over. Under her goggles, tears welled up in Zahra's eyes. She felt as if her heart was breaking watching the helpless creature and being unable to do anything to save it. Her vision blurred as her tears fell. "Ya Allah! What have we done to the earth?" She pulled off her goggles. "I can't watch this anymore."

Chapter 31

Yasser took his off as well and they both ran to Feel and hugged him like a long-lost friend. They were deeply touched by what they had just seen.

"Oh Feel," Zahra said. "This is so sad." The tears rolled down her cheeks freely.

"We can't just let stuff like that happen and do nothing!" Yasser said. "Humans can't go on destroying the earth like this."

"One of the first things you can do is not to buy anything made of ivory or elephant leather," Grandfather said. He had come to stand by them silently.

"But how can we help to save entire habitats?" Zahra asked. "We're just kids!"

"Look at how much we have learnt and how it's changed the way we see elephants. Maybe if we teach our friends and family more about elephants, they would appreciate how wonderful they are and work to keep them safe." Yasser added.

"There are places called sanctuaries and charities that work with governments to keep us safe," Feel said. "You can try to help them do their work better."

"I'm going to donate some of my pocket money every week to an elephant sanctuary!" declared Zahra.

"Me too!" Yasser said. "We'll save your relatives, Feel!"

"Thank you, children. InshaAllah you will be successful. Allah is my Protector and I rely on Him!" Feel said, pointing his trunk to the heavens to indicate that there is only one God.

Yasser took out his notebook again. He wanted to make sure they acted on the new information they had. He made a list of challenges and possible actions, leaving space for any new ideas they might come up with.

Chapter 32

They said their goodbyes to Feel, promising faithfully to remember what he had shown them. The sun was beginning to set and it was almost time for Maghrib prayers. The sky had turned a magnificent red and a brilliant orange. The birds were tweeting their evening glorifications.

Zahra and Yasser stood still, trying to capture the moment and preserve it in their minds. The day had taught them to stop and reflect on the beauty of Allah around them and nothing captured this more than the beautiful sunset and the constantly varying colours in the sky above them. At one moment it was filled with fiery oranges and reds and another with calmer pinks and purples.

Even if someone did not believe in Allah, the sunset would convince them that He exists, thought Zahra.

Yasser listened to the melodious tweeting of the birds all around them. "It sounds as though they are praying to Allah," he said.

"That is exactly what they are doing," said Grandfather.

"WHATEVER IS IN THE HEAVEN AND THE EARTH GLORIFIES ALLAH."

"SubhanAllah," Yasser responded, hoping to join in with their glorification.

As they walked back to the car, Yasser and Zahra could hardly believe they had experienced so many amazing things in just one day. It seemed like a week had passed since the morning! Grandfather drove through Hud Hud gates and as they gave the zoo a final glance from the back window of the car, there was a bright flash and they were driving back down their familiar street and heading home.

Grandfather parked in their driveway and switched off the car engine. "We're home, alhamdulillah!" he announced.

Yasser slipped off his seatbelt, but Zahra sat motionless in the car. She wasn't quite ready to return to the house; there was something playing on her mind.

"Grandfather, Feel said that Allah is our protector."

"Hmmm."

"We saw how Allah protected Prophet Salih and his followers from the terrible earthquake and Prophet Musa from Firawn. And you showed us how the spider's web is so fragile and that you cannot rely on anything but Allah." She hesitated. "But, **HOW** can we rely on Allah?"

Grandfather turned around in his seat to face his grandchildren. This was an important lesson; one they would continue to learn and build on throughout their lives. "Tawakkul, or relying on Allah, is an action of the heart," he said. "In happy times and in sad times, when you are frightened or excited, always know that Allah is your real protector and that He can help you."

"Knowing in your heart that Allah will always help you must give you a lot of peace and comfort," Yasser said, remembering his fear of spiders. "If you know deep down that Allah can do anything, then you'll always feel at ease, no matter what happens."

"That's right," nodded Grandfather. He was pleased that Yasser and Zahra were beginning to understand the meaning of tawakkul, but he wanted to give them examples that would be useful in their daily lives, so he cleared his throat and continued.

"The coronavirus that is spreading and affecting people is a humbling sign from Allah. The virus is microscopic, smaller than the smallest insect, yet it has affected all of humanity. We can choose to face it with or without tawakkul," he explained.

Zahra thought about how she had reacted to the pandemic. At different times she had been frightened, worried and uneasy. She had relied on the internet to help her with her work. She had relied on the government to make a sensible plan for the country. She had relied on the scientists to find a cure. She had placed her hope in so many different things, but she had not once stopped to ask Allah for help nor had she reflected on how it was only Allah who could truly protect them. *Face masks, social distancing and a strict hygiene routine will protect me*, she thought, *but only by the will of Allah*.

Yasser watched his sister; her eyebrows were narrowed and she seemed troubled by her thoughts. He gently leaned over and put his arm around her. "We need to hand over our worries and burdens to

Allah," he whispered. "He is on our side and He is always there to help us."

Zahra was surprised at Yasser's serious words. He would usually have made a joke, but his experience walking into the spider exhibition and relying on Allah seemed to have sobered him. She also remembered how the animals themselves had relied on their creator in all situations, not worrying about where their next meal would come from or how they should build their houses.

"You're right," she agreed. They knew they had learnt some very valuable lessons that day and had changed how they looked at the world. They both whispered a prayer to always have tawakkul and rely on Allah.

"Thank you, Grandfather!" Zahra said, reaching forward to give him a tight hug.

Yasser joined in. "Thank you," he echoed.

They both knew that there was no way to really thank their grandfather for the love, time, and attention he gave them. But what about the knowledge that he so painstakingly passed on to them? They could definitely find a way to thank him for that!

we can't sleep

Chapter 33

Zahra was tossing and turning in her bed. She had barely been able to focus on dinner or while getting ready to sleep. Her brain was buzzing from all that had happened in the day. Suddenly, she heard her bedroom door creak. She gasped; it was Yasser!

"Zahra," Yasser's whisper floated softly into the room. "Are you awake?"

"Yeah," she nodded in the darkness. "You can't sleep either?"

Yasser came and sat at the foot of her bed. She sat up and switched on her bedside lamp.

"I just keep thinking about all the animals we've seen today. We've learnt so much and I'm afraid if I don't do something about it, all the information will leak out of my ears!" Yasser admitted.

Zahra put her hand over her mouth to muffle her giggles. Her brother had such a funny way of expressing himself, but she knew exactly what he meant. It felt as though Allah had shown them new ways of understanding the world around them. The variety of animals, the lessons they had learnt from the Qur'an and the things Grandfather had taught them were not just interesting facts. They needed to **DO** something with their new-found knowledge; to take some kind of action.

Yasser and Zahra sat on her bed facing each other in the soft light and thought hard.

"Hmmm...perhaps our notebooks might help!" Zahra suggested.

"Great idea!" Yasser said in hushed whisper. He tiptoed to his room to grab his book, while Zahra took hers out of her satchel and opened it, ready to get started. As Zahra flipped through the pages, she relived the day through her notes and the pictures she had drawn.

She could see how Allah had designed all of His creation so deliberately. *Allah is truly al Musawwir. From Feel's footprint to Jamal's fur, nothing is there by accident*, Zahra thought. She could see how all of the animals, big or small, had a role to play on the planet. *Elephant footprints fill with water and turn into homes for little creatures. Spiders help to control insect population. Bees help all kinds of food to grow. Each and every one of them is a sign from Allah.*

Zahra closed her eyes and whispered a prayer. "Oh Allah, help me to recognise your signs and make me among the people who reflect." She looked at the Qur'an on her bedside table. How many times had it guided them through that special day? Through the different passages and verses, Allah had spoken to them directly. She picked up her Qur'an, kissed it and held it to her chest.

"I want to find out even more about what's inside you," she spoke to it, realising even more strongly how alive the book was.

Yasser watched from the doorway as Zahra whispered her du'a and cuddled her Qur'an. He loved that she had such a special relationship with the Holy Book and admired how she was determined to always improve.

We have learnt so much from the Qur'an today. Yasser thought about Abraha, who was arrogant like Firawn and the people of Thamud – all of whom had underestimated Allah's power. *Allah can protect whatever He wants to, like He protected the Kaaba, and He can destroy whoever He wants to, like the people of Thamud. He can guide whoever He wants to, like He guided the magicians of Egypt through the miracle of the snake.*

He thought of how fragile a spider's web was and smiled as he remembered how fearful he had been about entering the spider exhibition. *Animals are truly incredible,* he reflected, *it is our responsibility to look after them and make sure our actions do not harm them.* A smile crept over Yasser's face as he remembered how everything in the heavens and the earth glorified Allah – what a beautiful thought.

Zahra looked up at Yasser. She had an idea and as she explained her thoughts to Yasser, he nodded excitedly in agreement. He made some suggestions and slowly, working together, their plan began to take shape.

Chapter 34

Early the next morning, Grandfather was preparing a hearty breakfast of pancakes covered in the honey that reminded him of Nahla.

"Hmm, that's strange," he said to himself. "Yasser and Zahra are usually awake and buzzing around the house by now. I wonder what's happened?"

He went upstairs where all was still quiet. He made his way to Yasser's room and found it empty. Even more curious, he looked into Zahra's room; she was usually awake first. As he opened the door gently, he was confronted with a most intriguing sight.

Papers, stickers, felt tips, glue and coloured pencils littered the bedroom floor. There, huddled in the corner of the bed were both his grandchildren, fast asleep and clutching the fruit of their midnight efforts in their arms. Grandfather gently lifted their hands and picked up the book they had made during the night.

"Animals in the Qur'an Calendar – Thirty ways to act on our knowledge," he read out loud from the cover. "By Yasser and Zahra."

He looked through the book and saw pages of puzzles, crafts and activities all based on their trip to the zoo. Then he read the letter attached to the first page.

186

To all our friends around the world,

We've had the most wonderful adventures visiting the Animals of the Qur'an zoo! We learnt so much about our Creator, the Holy Qur'an, camels, snakes, bees, spiders, elephants, and lots about ourselves too. We want to share what we have learnt with all of you so we can journey together towards learning more about our wonderful Lord and His Word.

We thought the best way to do this was to make an activity book with lots of our favourite games and things to do. We hope you enjoy working through it as much as we enjoyed making it.

Through our journey, we have realised that animals are living creatures with feelings and connections to the spiritual and physical world. So let's be careful to look after them and be sincere in worshipping the One who created them and us!

We pray that we can all learn something new every day and grow up to be a generation that is kind to animals, reflects on Allah's signs and ponders over the Qur'an!

With lots of love, Yasser and Zahra

Grandfather placed the book and letter back on the bed and smiled at the sleeping children.

"**AMEEN**," he whispered. "**YA RABBAL ALAMEEN**."

Animals (in the) Qur'an calendar

By

Yasser & Zahra

day 1

raising awareness

We learnt so much on our trip to the zoo!

Did you know that 100 elephants are killed every day by poachers who want the elephant's ivory, leather and meat? We think that is terrible! Poaching, along with habitat loss, has meant that elephants really need our help! It's important to let other people know about the danger that elephants are in, so that we can all be careful about the products we buy and together we can save the elephants!

We're going to make a poster to raise awareness and stick it on our window so that people walking past can see! Will you join us? Here are some facts you could include:

- In Asia, elephants have disappeared from about 85% of their historic range.

- Less than 500,000 elephants remain in the wild.

- African elephant habitat has declined by over 50% since 1979, while Asian elephants are now restricted to just 15% of their original range.

day 2

donating to an animal charity

You can adopt an animal through many animal charities. After meeting Feel, we really wanted to adopt an elephant. It was really simple and WWF are going to send us an elephant cuddly toy, and lots of information about what we can do to save the elephants.

Visit https://support.wwf.org.uk/

THANK YOU

Yasser and Zahra

You're helping WWF to protect the future of wild elephants and to tackle some of the biggest environmental challenges facing our natural world today.
Thank you.

Paul De Ornellas
Chief Adviser – Wildlife, WWF-UK

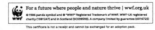

For a future where people and nature thrive | wwf.org.uk
© 1986 panda symbol and ® "WWF" Registered Trademark of WWF. WWF-UK registered charity (1081247) and in Scotland (SC039593). A company limited by guarantee (4016725)

This certificate is not a receipt and cannot be exchanged for an adoption pack.

day 3

Make a bee home in the garden

Nahla told us about how *bees* need safe homes to live in. We've decided to make a *bee* home in our garden. Here's how you can make one too:

Step 1: Take a wooden box and remove one side, or a you could cut the top off a large *plastic bottle*.

Step 2: Cut some *bamboo* sticks to the same length as the depth of your container.

Step 3: Pack the *bamboo* sticks or blocks of wood tightly into the box or *plastic bottle*.

Step 4: Attach a hook to the back of your *bee* house.

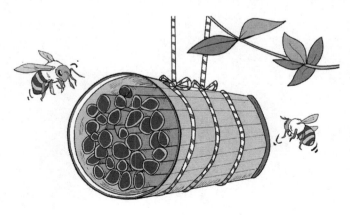

day 4

read verses of the qur'an and ponder over them

Grandfather showed us how important it is to reflect on the meaning of the verses of the Qur'an. We're going to try and do that today:

YASSER'S CHOICE OF VERSE:

"Do you not see that Allah is glorified by all those in the heavens and the earth, even the birds as they soar? Each knows their manner of prayer and glorification. And Allah has perfect knowledge of all they do." (24:41)

How does that verse make you feel?

_____

_____

_____

_____

_____

ZAHRA'S CHOICE OF VERSE:

"And were you to count the blessings of Allah, you could not number them. Truly Allah is Forgiving, Merciful." (16:18)

Have you ever tried to count your blessings? What happened?

_____

_____

_____

_____

_____

Why do you think Allah uses His names Forgiving and Merciful here?

_____

_____

_____

_____

_____

day 5

Matching game!

Have you been paying attention? Can you match the animal to their Arabic name and their story in the Qur'an?

Elephant	Ankabut	The people of Thamud
Camel	Nahla	Abraha and his army
Spider	Hud Hud	Honey is a cure
Bee	Feel	The house of the spider
Hoopoe	Naaqa	Prophet Sulayman

day 6

find out about the story of Prophet Sulayman and the ant

Although we've learnt a lot about elephants, camels, spiders and bees, there are over thirty animals mentioned in the Qur'an and we want to know about all of them! Today we are going to find out more about Prophet Sulayman and the ant.

"Until, when they came upon the valley of the ants, an ant said, 'O ants, enter your homes so that you do not be crushed by Sulayman and his soldiers while they do not feel it.' Quran 27:18

What have you found out about the story?

day 7

Make something with honey

Honey is super tasty! We've decided to surprise Grandfather by making him some honeycomb! We'll need our mum's help though!

Here's how we'll do it, inshaAllah!

INGREDIENTS: 1 tablespoon baking soda sifted, 1 1/4 cups white granulated sugar, 1/2 cup honey, Pinch of fine sea salt, 1 teaspoon pure vanilla extract

INSTRUCTIONS: Line a baking sheet with parchment and have it nearby. A silicon spatula also comes in handy with this recipe. In a large pot pour in the sugar, honey and salt. Heat the sugar mixture to 295 degreesF, for about 3 minutes, stirring it with a silicon spatula. The mixture will turn an autumn-like brown. Turn off the heat and then immediately add the vanilla extract and baking soda. The mixture will foam up quite a bit, continue stirring until the baking soda completely dissolves. Quickly pour the honeycomb mixture onto a sheet of parchment. Allow it to cool completely before touching it, about 2 minutes. Then.....ENJOY!

day 8

animals in the qur'an word search

There are thirty-one animals mentioned in the Qur'an. Can you find them in this word search?

Q	U	A	I	L	E	P	E	E	H	S
W	M	O	S	Q	U	I	T	O	D	N
O	O	F	R	O	G	O	A	T	O	A
L	T	C	R	O	W	B	E	E	G	K
F	H	M	A	E	W	E	M	U	L	E
S	A	P	E	L	I	C	E	R	D	Y
R	N	H	S	I	F	L	Y	P	O	L
E	T	C	P	I	G	L	I	O	N	O
D	C	A	T	T	L	E	L	E	K	C
I	O	M	H	O	R	S	E	T	E	U
P	W	E	H	O	O	P	O	E	Y	S
S	E	L	E	P	H	A	N	T	W	T
W	O	R	M	Y	U	S	D	R	I	B

day 9

Spot the difference

We've kept our eyes peeled throughout the trip to the zoo! Can you spot the five differences in the pictures below?

day 10

tawakkul

When Abraha wanted to attack the Kaaba he stole 200 of Abdul Muttalib's camels. When Abdul Muttalib found out, he went to visit Abraha. Abraha thought that Abdul Muttalib had come to try and convince him not to attack the Kaaba, but instead he asked Abraha to return the camels. Abraha was shocked and asked Abdul Muttalib why he had not asked about the Kaaba! Surely that was more important. What did Abdul Muttalib reply?

What does that teach you about tawakkul? How can you rely on Allah in your life?

_____

_____

_____

_____

_____

day 11

remember tawakkul

Yasser loves making posters! Here's one he made to help him remember to always have tawakkul. Why not make one too?

WHOEVER *relies on* **ALLAH**, *then* HE IS SUFFICIENT FOR HIM.

(Qur'an 65:3)

day 12

Stop and think

When we were walking to the camels, we realised that we are usually too busy to stop and look at all the beauty Allah has created all around us. Pausing helped us to feel calm and appreciate Allah's blessings.

Why not try it yourself? Take a walk through the forest and listen to the sounds of all the animals – they are all praising Allah! Take pictures of Allah's beautiful creation. Don't forget to take your notebooks!

day 13

Zahra's Woven Spider's Web

I had so much fun meeting Ankaboot! It was truly amazing to watch her spin a web! Now I want to make one of my own so that I can remember the verse she told us about (and also to try and scare Yasser!! hehe!)

You need: Glue, three lollipop sticks, and yarn.

Instructions:

1. Glue three lollipop sticks together,

2. Cut a long piece of yarn and tie one end to a lollipop stick.

3. Wrap the yarn around each lollipop stick and keep going round in a circle until almost all your yarn is used up. Tie one last knot.

4. Attach the verse, "The frailest of houses is the house of the spider."

The frailest of houses is the house of the spider

205

day 14

Yasser's Camel Maze

I had so much fun making this maze for Jamal to reach the water! Have a go! I've tried to make it tricky!

day 15

Provide fresh water to animals

You don't need to go to a jungle or rainforest to be kind to animals! Animals are everywhere, in your back garden, the park, or any outdoor space! Like us, animals need fresh water to survive. Why not leave a bowl of fresh water for them every day? Quenching the thirst of an animal is a very good deed!

Where will you put yours?

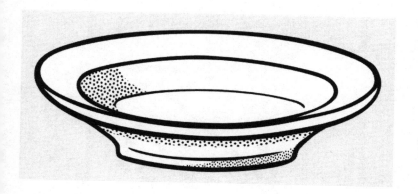

day 16

Make a qiblah pointer

Feel told us an amazing story about how Allah protected the Kaaba from Abraha and his army. It made us remember that Allah is the Lord of the Kaaba! SubhanAllah! We turn to the Kaaba at least five times a day to pray. Having a qiblah helps us remember to have direction and focus in our lives.

We've decided to make a qiblah pointer to stick on the ceiling in our bedrooms. It shows us the direction to face for prayer and also reminds us that we should always focus on Allah!

All you need is card or paper, coloured pens or pencils and some scissors!

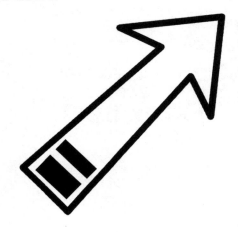

day 17

think about how we were made

We've been thinking a lot about how Allah created the animals and the beautiful world around us. That got us thinking...what about us? Has Allah created us in a special way too?

Look in the mirror, really look hard. What can you see? Spend time looking at the blood vessels in your eyes and the way you make your fingers move and how you can run and jump. Think about how Allah created you from nothing and gave you a mind to think and worship Him! You are so special!

Write down your reflections here:

_____

_____

_____

_____

_____

day 18

animals in the qur'an Crossword

We love the Qur'an and we love crosswords! What better way to find out where animals are mentioned in the Qur'an!

The clues are references to verses in the Qur'an - Have fun!

ACROSS		DOWN	
1	2:67	1	5:31
3	2:26	2	12:13
4	22:73	5	74:51
7	20:20	6	16:8
8	18:18	7	29:41
9	2:260	9	16:68
11	88:17	10	31:19
16	105:1	12	27:18
		13	54:7
		14	2:65
		15	2:51

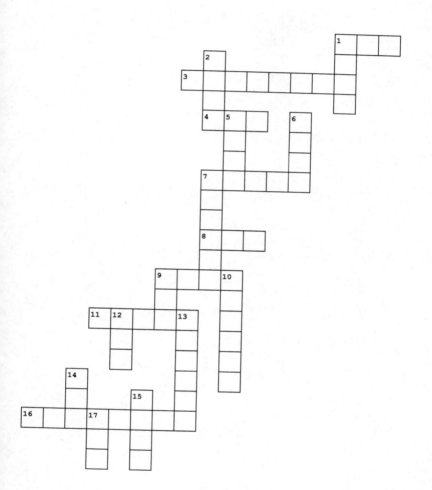

211

day 19

Yasser's animal jokes

Q: Why are elephants so wrinkled?
A: Did you ever try to iron one?

Q: What kind of bee is a sore loser?
A: A cryba-bee

Q: What was the elephant's favourite sport?
A: Squash

Q: What do you call a horse that lives next door?
A: A neigh-bour!

Q: Why do cows have hooves instead of feet?
A: Because they lactose!

Q: What did the sushi say to the bee?
A: Wassabee!

Q: What does a bee style his hair with?
A: A honeycomb

Q: Why did the spider get a job at Google?
A: She was a great web designer.

day 20

Plant a tree

Looking to the future, we realised that we have to take responsibility for the resources we use. We can make the world a cleaner and safer place for animals by planting trees and protecting their habitats!

The Holy Prophet said: "Every single Muslim that cultivates or plants anything of which humans, animals or birds may eat from is counted as charity towards them on his behalf."

day 21

Product Check

We found out that animals can really suffer because some of the products that humans use that are harmful for them. This could be because they are poisonous or because to make them, humans destroy the homes and habitats of many animals.

We're going to have a look around the house to see if we can identify any ingredients in cleaning products or food packages that harms animals -so we know not to buy those things again!

day 22

finish Zahra's poem about the People of thamud

Zahra started writing a poem about the people of Thamud. Can you help her finish it off?

The people of Thamud,

They were not very good,

They didn't listen to Prophet Salih,

even though they should,

Instead, they worshipped the idol,

Followed their forefather's cycle,

Even after they asked for the she-camel's arrival,

_____

_____

_____

_____

day 23

recite the morning and evening glorifications

Whatever is in the heavens and the earth glorifies Allah! Join in with these glorifications for the morning and evening: Translation from duas.org

أَصْبَحْـنا وَأَصْبَـحْ المُـلْكُ لله رَبِّ العـالَمـين

The morning has come to me and the whole universe belongs to Allah, the Lord of the worlds

اللّهُـمَّ إِنِّي أَسْأَلُكَ خَـيْرَ هـذا اليَوْم

O Allah, I ask of you the good of the day,

فَـتْحَهُ ، وَنَصْـرَهُ ، وَنـورَهُ وَبَـرَكَتَـهُ ، وَهُـداهُ

it's success and aid and it's light, blessings and guidance

وَأَعـوذُ بِـكَ مِـنْ شَـرِّ ما فيهِ وَشَـرِّ ما بَعْـدَه

and I seek refuge from the evil in it (this day) and from the evil of that which is to come later.

أَمْسَيْنَا وَأَمْسَى الْمُلْكُ لِلَّهِ رَبِّ الْعَالَمِين

The evening has come to me and the whole universe belongs to Allah who is The Lord of the worlds.

اللَّهُمَّ إِنِّي أَسْأَلُكَ خَيْرَ هَذِهِ اللَّيْلَةَ

O Allah, I ask of you the good of the night,

فَتْحَهَا وَنَصْرَهَا وَنُورَهَا وَبَرَكَتَهَا وَهُدَاهَا

it's success and aid and it's light, blessings and guidance

وَأَعُوذُ بِكَ مِنْ شَرِّ مَا فِيهَا وَشَرِّ مَا بَعْدَهَا

and I seek refuge from the evil in this night and from the evil of that which is to come later.

day 24

make an animal bookmark!

Camel facts

Grandfather is always encouraging us to read! "Iqra!" he says when we ask him how he knows so much!

We're making these snazzy animal bookmarks which we are going to fill with interesting facts we have learnt!

Won't you join us?

Elephant facts

day 25

Yasser's Worry Spinner

Sometimes when I feel worried, I don't know how to calm down. So I decided to make this worry spinner so that next time I feel worried or overwhelmed I can spin the spinner and do one of the activities I've thought of in advance!

Here's some ideas I am going to add: Perform wudhu, read a book, play with Lego, write down how I feel, do some breathing exercises, make dua, look out of my window and recite Ayatul Kursi!

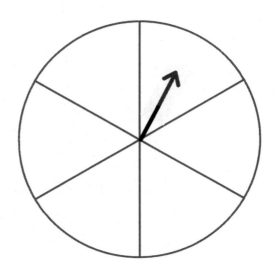

day 26

descriptions of the qur'an

One of our main goals after we visited the zoo was to understand the Qur'an more!

We're going to have a look at these verses and see what they tell us about the nature of the Qur'an. Why don't you have a go with us and send us your thoughts!

QUR'ANIC REFERENCES:
2:185, 5:15, 16:89, 6:34, 6:115

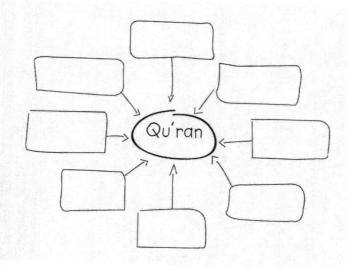

day 27

Snake Magic

Remember when we saw Prophet Musa's staff turn into a snake? THAT WAS AMAZING!

We've tried to recreate the experience to remind us of Allah's power with this captivating experiment!

Step 1: Cut out a circle from a piece of tissue paper and draw a spiral snake inside it.

2. We decorated out snake with a zigzag pattern and added some eyes and smile. You can decorate yours however you like, then cut along the spiral.

3. Now for the magic! Rub a plastic ruler quite hard and fast for about thirty seconds on a scarf or sweater made of wool.

4. Then touch the snake's head with the ruler. The snake should uncoil and rise up!

223

day 28

Make a jigsaw puzzle

We realised that we are all connected and what we do makes a difference to the world, whether positive or negative. Feel's footprints made a home for little animals and if it wasn't for spiders the whole world would be covered insects! We're going to make a jigsaw puzzle to show how everything is connected!

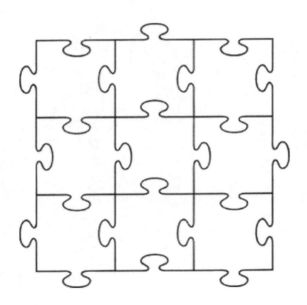

day 29

draw the other half of the snake

Allah is the best Designer! We're going to have some fun today trying to draw the other half of Thu'baan!

day 30

Yasser and Zahra's quiz!

We're going to end our thirty days of activities by having a quiz to see how much we've learnt! Why not join in and send your answers to us by email!

Question 1: Which surah is the story of Prophet Salih and the she-camel in?

Question 2: What was the name of Prophet Musa's brother?

Question 3: How can camels sit on the hot desert ground?

Question 4: What is Grandfather's favourite treat?

Question 5: Why does Yasser always feel better after performing wudhu?

Question 6: Who is Hud Hud?

Question 7: What is the world's largest land mammal?

Question 8: What is the name of the Abyssinian King who wanted to destroy the Kaaba?

Question 9: How did the spider save Prophet Muhammad in the cave?

Question 10: Write the word for "snake" in Arabic

Question 11: What was the name of the Prophet's camel?

Question 12: What happened to the people of Thamud?

Question 13: Name three things that happened to Firawn after he refused to let Prophet Musa and the Bani Israel go.

Question 14: How do you say "Welcome" in Arabic?

Question 15: How many muscle's are there in an elephant's   trunk?

Question 16: How do snakes smell with their tongues?

Question 17: What does "Dhul Jalaali wal Ikram" mean?

Question 18: What does a queen bee do?

Question 19: Who is older - Yasser or Zahra?

Question 20: In which surah and verse does Allah inspire bees with knowledge?

More of Yasser and Zahra's adventures:
Available from: www.sunbehindthecloud.com